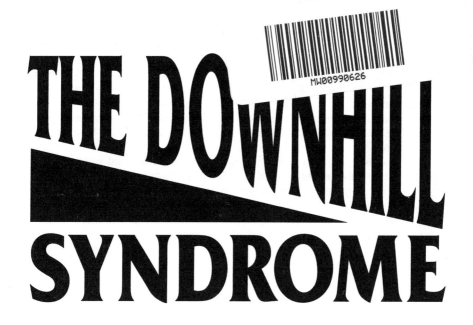

THE DOWNHILL SYNDROME

DR. PAVEL YUTSIS
DR. MORTON WALKER

A DR. MORTON WALKER HEALTH BOOK

Avery Publishing Group
Garden City Park, New York

The therapeutic procedures in this book are based on the training, personal experiences, and research of the author. Because each person and situation is unique, the author and publisher urge the reader to check with a qualified health professional before using any procedure where there is any question to appropriateness.

The publisher does not advocate the use of any particular diet or health program, but believes the information presented in this book should be available to the public.

Because there is always some risk involved, the author and publisher are not responsible for any adverse effects or consequences resulting from the use of any of the suggestions, preparations, or procedures in this book. Please do not use the book if you are unwilling to assume the risk. Feel free to consult with a physician or other qualified health professional. It is a sign of wisdom, not cowardice, to seek a second or third opinion.

Library of Congress Cataloging-in-Publication Data
Yutsis, Pavel.
    The downhill syndrome : if nothing's wrong, why do I feel so bad? /
Pavel Yutsis, Morton Walker.
        p.   cm.
    Includes bibliographical references and index.
    ISBN 0-89529-758-2 (pbk.)
        1. Chronic fatigue syndrome—Popular works. I. Walker, Morton.
II. Title.
    RB 150.F37Y88   1997
    616'.0478—dc2   96-5487
                                                                 CIP

Printed in the United States of America

10 9   8   7   6   5   4   3   2

CONTENTS

Foreword

Preface

Part I   Toward An Understanding of the Downhill Syndrome

1. Tracking Down a Mysterious Fatigue Epidemic   3
2. Signs and Symptoms of the Downhill Syndrome   9
3. Searching for the Causes of the Downhill Syndrome   17
4. Diagnosing the Downhill Syndrome   25
5. Metabolic Immunodepression   31

Part II   Viruses As Cofactors of the Downhill Syndrome

6. Chronic Epstein-Barr Virus   45
7. The Cytomegalovirus (CMV)   53
8. The Human Herpesvirus-VI (HHV-6)   59
9. Human Retroviruses As Disease Factor   65
10. Potential Cures for Viral Infections   71

Part III   Other Cofactors

11. The Factor of Yeast in CFIDS   79
12. Dental Amalgam Toxicity   87
13. How Heavy Metals and Chemicals Poison The Body   95
14. How To Eliminate Heavy Metals and Chemical Pollutants From Your Body   105
15. Disease Symptoms From Allergies   111

16. Tests and Treatments For Allergies   121
17. Underactive Thyroid —Another Contributing Factor   135
18. Parasites As Disease Factors   145
19. Moving Upward From the Downhill Syndrome   157
     References   165
     Index   185

FOREWORD

In this era, we are undergoing profound changes in our view of the health-disease continuum, because a radically new philosophy of caring for the chronically ill is rapidly evolving all over the world. Finally, the medical community and patients are coming to recognize that the concept of reversing chronic disease with synthetic chemicals is fundamentally flawed.

Until now, the vast majority of practicing physicians have been close-minded to the fact that injured tissues heal with nutrients, not drugs. Drugs are poisons that are devised by pharmaceutical peddlers. Synthetic drugs cannot facilitate the healing process.

The star wars medical technology that we're exposed to in current health-care practice allows doctors to cope with acute illness in ways that were unimaginable when I started my medical studies almost four decades ago. But this technology has utterly failed in reversing chronic ecological, nutritional, immunological, and stress-related disorders.

The new, improved, and emerging model of medicine—more humanistic (wholistic) in its concept—calls for the philosophy of health used by the ancients combined with twenty-first century medical science. Those ancient African, Chinese, Egyptian, and Indian healing artists emphasized the need for supporting a sick body with nutrients, prayer, and natural plant-derived remedies. Many healing agents were herbal substances that co-evolved with human biologic processes over millions of years. The sad truth of our times is that such natural therapies are quite effective in most cases for reversing chronic health disorders, but they have been ignored by conventionally practiced medicine.

Fortunately, now we have The *Downhill Syndrome,* a book about the intricate collective causes of chronic fatigue and immune dysfunction, jointly authored by Pavel "Paul" I. Yutsis, M.D., and Morton Walker, D.P.M. Their collective effort provides an outstanding contribution to our understanding of the health and disease continuum that I mentioned. My prediction is that this volume will have a long and well-used life. It is dedicated to the service of patients suffering from the variety of symptoms making up the all-inclusive chronic fatigue syndrome, and to the physicians who wish to help these patients.

Dr. Yutsis, a kind and humanistic practicing physician, brings to this work an extraordinary depth of clinical perspective. He has devoted thousands of hours to listening to his patients, whose immune systems had been destroyed by long-term drug therapies. He understands the true cost of synthetic drugs on human biology.

Dr. Walker has had enormous experience in breaking new journalistic ground in innovative therapies. He writes columns for no less than six natural health clinical journals and magazines about innovative biologics.

In this book, the two authors focus on the issues of chronic fatigue and immune dysfunction with clarity and precision. Utterly uninhibited by the cluttered medical jargon that fills hundreds of journals, this book "tells it like it is." They hold nothing back.

The many issues related to the Downhill Syndrome are discussed with an engaging depth of perspective. Dr. Yutsis and Dr. Walker offer discussions of invading viruses, metabolic immunodepression, the association of parasites with yeast in the bowel ecosystem, plus the insidious damage to human enzymes caused by chemical pollutants, heavy metals, and environmental pollutants. Subjects like these are especially valuable to both patients and practitioners of the emerging field of preventive medicine.

In my own book, *RDA: Rats, Drugs, and Assumptions,* I try to lay bare many of the documented deceptions in medical statistics, and have found that most of them were actually intended. With extensive citations, I show how results of valid medical research are often deliberately distorted to promote long-term use of drugs of dubious value. I also try to show the deep prejudice of practitioners of drug medicine against natural, nondrug, nontoxic therapies. But the highbrow scientists in the United States rarely take the next step:

speak courageously and forcefully against the utter futility of trying to solve health problems caused by yet more synthetic chemicals. Instead, that task has been taken up by courageous men of good will: Dr. Paul Yutsis and Dr. Morton Walker.

Majid Ali, M.D.,
Associate Professor of Pathology,
College of Physicians and Surgeons of Columbia University

PREFACE

Millions of people living in Western industrialized countries are dragging themselves through life, sick with a wide variety of debilitating symptoms. In addition to suffering from overwhelming fatigue, they have aching muscles and joints, throbbing heads, swollen lymph glands, and droopy eyelids. They also have problems concentrating and remembering. They feel emotionally drained, have ongoing depression, lethargy, ever-present anxiety, recurrent sore throats, frequent sniffles and symptoms of colds, and endure the discomforts of gastrointestinal distress and debilitating allergies, among others.

Victims who report such symptoms might be labeled "the walking weary," and say they are "sick and tired of being sick and tired."

"I feel like a Raggedy Ann doll with the stuffing knocked out," one patient told a reporter for *The New York Times*. "It's as if I have an endless bout of flu with the added mental confusion of Alzheimer's disease," said another patient.

What had once been considered a vague and seemingly incurable series of health problems is now recognized by the conventional medical community as a true disabling disease. Because of the diversity of symptoms, the disease has been labeled with a variety of names. Until 1994, it was called *mononucleosis, chronic fatigue syndrome, chronic mononucleosis-like syndrome, chronic Epstein-Barr virus infection, cytomegaloviral disease, Iceland disease,* and *epidemic neuromyasthenia.* For two decades, the British labeled this series of health problems myalgic encephalomyelitis, and the Japanese referred to these symptoms as low natural killer cell syndrome.

Unaffected and uninformed people have disparaged the disease with idiomatic names such as yuppie flu and yuppie fever.

Physicians who once considered the individual's chronic fatigue as a secondary manifestation of depression now recognize it as the very real and very serious disease, chronic fatigue and immune dysfunction syndrome, or CFIDS. We have given this condition another simpler and more descriptive name: The Downhill Syndrome.

The Downhill Syndrome is estimated by the American Academy of Environmental Medicine to affect 24 million Americans, 6 million Canadians, 5 million Australians, 9 million residents of Great Britain, and uncounted millions of others in Europe, South America, and Asia.

Based on personal medical research plus clinical reports from some 1,800 wholistic, environmental, and biological physicians, we believe that there is an ever-growing spread of the Downhill Syndrome among the populations of Western industrialized nations. Its rampant occurrence stems from society's excessive use of high technology, which produces immune suppression and associated immunological disease symptoms.

This book offers a comprehensive look at what is currently known about the probable causes and potential cures of the Downhill Syndrome. We explain the reasons for various symptoms, and offer tests that may be self-administered to check for particular illnesses associated with the Downhill Syndrome. In addition, we discuss therapies that are proving to be effective.

The good news is that patients suffering from the Downhill Syndrome have been treated successfully with methods pioneered by two wholistic medical specialty groups, the American College for Advancement in Medicine (ACAM) and the American Academy of Environmental Medicine (AAEM).

Since 1992, ACAM has adopted Dr. Yutsis's program for permanently correcting CFIDS. By writing this book, we hope to bring this important and hopeful information to CFIDS patients and their conventional physicians.

Paul I. Yutsis, M.D.,
Brooklyn, New York

Morton Walker, D.P.M.,
Stamford, Connecticut

PART I

TOWARD AN UNDERSTANDING OF THE DOWNHILL SYNDROME

"Chronic fatigue is emerging as
the most dominant health disorder of our time."

—Majid Ali, M.D., Associate Professor of Pathology,
*College of Physicians and Surgeons
of Columbia University, New York*

This section will familiarize you with the basics of the Downhill Syndrome, and help you understand the intricate mechanisms that are involved in its development. The authors will explore the search for the causes of this syndrome, as well as its warning signs and symptoms, and a variety of diagnostic tools that will significantly aid in uncovering "the mysterious fatigue." Finally, the main source of almost all the signs and symptoms of the Downhill Syndrome will be explored, so you know how to cope with them.

1

Tracking Down a Mysterious Fatigue Epidemic

In 1984, a fatiguing ailment struck Incline Village, a small resort community at Lake Tahoe, Nevada. Then, in late 1985, a similar fatiguing ailment struck the tiny Nevada ranching town of Yerington. Out of a total population of 1,243, one hundred thirty-four people were hit with unexplained, debilitating fatigue that was accompanied with muscle and joint pains, headaches, sore throats, painful lymph nodes, and other symptoms. At the time, doctors labelled their patients' collective signs and symptoms as "chronic fatigue syndrome."

THE MEDICAL DETECTIVE WORK OF DR. PAUL CHENEY

Someone who did significant medical detective work on the two Nevada sites was Paul R. Cheney, M.D., Ph.D. , who lived in Incline Village and is now medical director of The Cheney Clinic in Charlotte, North Carolina. In the early 1980s, Dr. Cheney had joined Dan Peterson's newly opened general medical practice.

The village, a "Carmel-by-the-Sea" type of town with upscale condominiums and lakefront mansions, is a resort community whose business people did not want to hear about any widespread illness. Nevertheless, many of its residents came into Dr. Cheney and Dr. Peterson's office complaining of viral symptoms typically found in mononucleosis. They suffered from sore throats, swollen lymph glands, aching muscles, weakness in the limbs or partial paralysis, blackouts, vivid nightmares, spatial disorientation, and memory loss.

3

Although the classic blood test for mononucleosis, which measures a clotting reaction, invariably came up negative for these patients, Drs. Cheney and Peterson treated their patients for this disease. They ordered bed rest and prescribed analgesics to control pain and salt gargles for throat discomfort, but the patients failed to get well no matter what treatment was tried.

Searching the medical literature for clues, the doctors finally came upon papers written separately by Stephen Straus, M.D., head of the medical virology section of the National Institute of Allergy and Infectious Diseases in Washington, D.C., and James F. Jones, M.D., now with the National Jewish Center for Immunology and Respiratory Medicine in Denver. The articles, published in the 1985 *Annals of Internal Medicine,* described several dozen patients who suffered from recurrent or persistent fatigue, fever, headaches, and depression. Nearly all of these referred patients showed elevated levels of antibodies to the Epstein-Barr virus (EBV).

The EBV, named after its discoverers, twentieth-century British virologists M. Anthony Epstein, M.D., and Yvonne M. Barr, M.D., is a member of the herpes family of viruses, which brings humankind chicken pox, cold sores, genital lesions, shingles, and other ailments.

A Negative Reaction to Cheney's Findings

When Dr. Cheney reported his suspicions about EBV as the causative organism for chronic fatigue syndrome to the federal Centers for Disease Control and Prevention (CDC), that agency, which is responsible for keeping the American population healthy, sent two of its epidemiological investigators to check his findings. Jon Kaplan, M.D., and Gary Holmes, M.D., arrived at Incline Village in September, 1985. Eight months later, the two epidemiologists issued a critical report implying that Dr. Cheney was just using his imagination, and that nothing unusual had happened. They further insinuated that most patients were suffering with a psychosomatic disorder or had outright mental illness. Physicians throughout the nation were urged not to diagnose any patients as having chronic EBV syndrome until more "definable and treatable" conditions such as anxiety and depression had been ruled out.

In press hearings, Dr. Holmes made some unkind statements about the diagnostic skills of Dr. Cheney. "I would not take what he was telling you about patients at face value," he said. "I think that's true of a lot of physicians, especially private physicians, who get caught up. They think they notice something, then they start seeing it everywhere."

A New Approach

Still, Dr. Cheney persisted. Armed with a background as a researcher for the Center for Disease Control and Prevention in Atlanta, he added some infectious disease research. He suspected that the recently appearing chronic fatigue syndrome was an immune system disorder brought on by EBV or several other viruses that were attacking the patient simultaneously.

In the summer of 1988, Dr. Cheney asked Elaine DeFreitas, Ph.D., an immunologist at Wistar Institute (a part of the University of Pennsylvania and the nation's premier research laboratory for HIV) to examine thirty samples of blood taken from his patients, and twenty others gathered from the general population. Dr. DeFreitas found that of Dr. Cheney's group, 77 percent contained a distinctive piece of genetic material found in a particular virus. None of the other blood samples contained the same viral gene.

Dr. DeFreitas had used a new and sensitive technique for detecting viruses—the polymerase chain reaction (PCR). Employing PCR, she detected a unique gene present in the patients' blood samples for a viral strain identified as the human T-lymphotropic virus (HTLV).

ADDITIONAL RESEARCH

Later, Dr. Cheney and Dr. DeFreitas were joined in their investigations by pediatrician David Bell, M.D., from the tiny town of Lyndonville in upstate New York. After nearly three years of research, they reported that HTLV takes several forms that are represented by the Roman numerals I, II, and III. For example, HTLV-I is linked to a rare form of leukemia and to multiple sclerosis, while HTLV-II has an association with the blood disorder known as hairy cell leukemia. HTLV-III has been redesignated as the now-common HIV, better known as the virus that causes acquired immune deficiency syndrome (AIDS).

HTLV-II, like the AIDS virus, survives only in body fluids such as blood and semen. But the illness the researchers were studying is not transmitted by an exchange of body fluids, as is AIDS. Thus, they reasoned, HTLV-II was probably not the causative agent of CFIDS.

Using another technique called *in situ* hybridization, Dr. DeFreitas checked for newly minted ribonucleic acid (RNA) from HTLV-II. In blood samples from healthy carriers of HTLV-II, no suspicious gene was found. But for six of twelve patients suffering from CFIDS, the RNA of HTLV-II was churning out copies of itself.

Dr. Cheney has continued his investigative work, compiling a statistical analysis of abnormal metabolites in Downhill Syndrome patients. To date, he maintains a database of over 2,500 such patients.

MORE PIONEERS

In 1986, Dr. Bell got involved in researching the syndrome then labeled "yuppie flu," because the patients who complained of chronic fatigue in the village of Lyndonville were far from yuppies. He and his wife Karen, an infectious disease specialist, are the only two physicians practicing in this town of 1,000, which is surrounded by apple orchards and cornfields. By the end of that year, nearly 10 percent of Lyndonville's population had been laid low by the ailment. Dr. Bell, a pediatrician, declared, "In Lyndonville there were no yuppies, just a lot of sick kids and adults."

They suffered from the mystery malaise, which often started with a distinct flu-like illness, leaving patients sick, weak, and extremely tired for at least six months. It often included swollen glands, muscle and joint pains, sore throat, dizziness, and headaches, plus problems in concentration and memory. The symptoms waxed and waned, worsening after exertion, infections, and stress. Dr. Bell eliminated other possibilities, including mononucleosis, multiple sclerosis, lupus erythematosis, depression, and AIDS. His patients did not die without treatment, but they frequently lingered with their mysterious malaise for three to five years.

A FAMILY OF SUFFERERS

Among Dr. David Bell's patients were three of the four children of Mrs. Jean Pollard. A wicked flu-like illness, plus swollen glands, fevers, aches, and rashes beset Hannah, Libby, and Megan Pollard.

"My kids were just lying in the fetal position on the floor. They wouldn't even get up and walk into the kitchen for food. They couldn't stand the light. Even the light from the TV was too bright," Mrs. Pollard told Dr. Bell.

Libby, now age twenty-one, literally crawled from room to room. "We had such bad headaches in the morning, we couldn't even raise our heads," she says. "We were too tired to get up and too tired to sleep."

The Pollards learned that another family in Lyndonville, the Duncansons, had several children with the same symptoms. Jean Pollard didn't worry much, though—she was the office manager for the town's only physicians, the Bells. David Bell assured Mrs. Pollard that whatever it was, the illness would probably clear up in a week or two.

"It looked like a typical virus," Dr. Bell says. "But a week later, they weren't getting any better. And then the week after that they weren't better. By the third week, I knew we weren't dealing with a regular virus."

Meanwhile, more children and adults got sick. Some were too sick to go to school or work; others managed to drag through daily routines.

The Bells spent Thanksgiving of 1985 hunched over medical books, trying to find an answer. Nothing fit. Later, they brought the Pollards and Duncansons into their office and searched for common denominators. Had the children handled dead animals? Played with turtles?

Dr. Bell heard whispers that the children were suffering from hysteria, but never seriously entertained that thought himself. "I'd known all those kids for years and years, and they were just plain sick," he says.

What's more, the afflicted townspeople stayed sick for months, or even years. While Dr. Bell has continued the search for a cause, most of the nearly 500 patients he saw have improved, but few have recovered entirely. He's in contact with one young woman who has sinced moved to New York City.

Alison Pollard, now age twenty-three, the oldest of the Pollard daughters, tells a typical Downhill Syndrome story. She got sick about a year after her three younger sisters and was bedridden for seven years.

On a day that's obviously going to be bad for her, the young woman, who recently graduated from college, explains: "All of a sudden this feeling comes over my body and I feel like if I don't lie down right away, I'm going to die. The energy just drains out of my body in five minutes." Alison says she doesn't want the Downhill Syndrome to rule her life: "I lead a pretty normal life. I just keep my pains to myself . . . . Unless they find a cure, it's just something I'll have to live with."

AN EVER-GROWING HEALTH PROBLEM

Outbreaks continue to occur. There have been outbreaks of the condition in such diverse areas as Vancouver, Mexico City, Madrid, Rio de Janeiro, London, Paris, Amsterdam, and Tel Aviv. Groups of young adults in major American cities, the entire memberships of various metropolitan and suburban social clubs, civic associations, church congregations, and other organized groups have experienced the disease symptoms.

"Whatever it is, it seems to be growing in frequency," says Anthony L. Komaroff, M.D., director of general medicine at Brigham and Women's Hospital in Boston, whose group has studied more than 6,000 New England patients suffering from the Downhill Syndrome. "Literally every time I say to a friend that I'm studying this illness, and then describe it, he or she will reply, 'Oh, my God. My niece has it,' or 'my neighbor,' or 'my boss.'"

The puzzle and the scientific research continues. As yet, there is no unified theory as to why the outbreaks occurred, since a sole explanation pointing to viruses turned out to be insufficient. As we'll see in later chapters, researchers have uncovered a variety of sources for the Downhill Syndrome, and there are not only new theories, there are new treatments and new hope, as well.

2.

SIGNS AND SYMPTOMS OF THE DOWNHILL SYNDROME

A s we've already seen, the primary symptom of the Downhill Syndrome is fatigue. But the kind of fatigue demonstrated is markedly different from what most people recognize as tiredness. If you were a victim of the Downhill Syndrome, you would welcome any kind of regular fatigue over what you currently experience. Four of the Lake Tahoe sufferers demonstrate what we mean.

FOUR DOWNHILL SYNDROME FATIGUE SUFFERERS

First, there is Sandy Schmidt, a community leader, sports enthusiast, and manager of her husband's Incline Village estate-planning business. Mrs. Schmidt had just finished running the San Francisco marathon when the illness caught up with her. "At first I thought it was the deep tiredness of post-race fatigue," she says. "But it was so exaggerated. I was sleeping fifteen hours a day and getting worse. I'd try to stay up, but just couldn't concentrate or think or work."

The longest she felt well enough to be a business woman again was only a month. Then she would be forced to collapse into bed for weeks. After spending a year and a half controlled by fatigue, Mrs. Schmidt began to feel better. She now feels like her old energetic self, and has resumed running once more.

Then, there is Joyce Reynolds, a bank teller in north Lake Tahoe. After contracting this devastating disease, she became, in her own words, "a total recluse." Even as simple a thing as going to the movies with her husband landed Mrs. Reynolds in bed for days at a time.

Next, there is Gerald Kennedy, who taught auto mechanics and drafting at the Tahoe-Truckee Unified High School. He had a flawless record of twenty-four years of unbroken attendance at his job, which was fortunate, because the accumulated sick leave helped to support his family for the two rocky years he could not work out of the sheer inability to get out of bed. "It's been a new experience, I'll tell you," he says. "People were skeptical about my illness. After a while you feel a little better and you start questioning yourself. That's when you try doing something—maybe drive out, sit by the lake in a lawn chair and fish for a couple of hours—and pay the penalty for the next week. It's like riding a roller coaster."

"Yeah, or a picket fence," added Gloria Baker of Riverside, California, who teaches at the same high school as Mr. Kennedy. Following a year of bed rest, Mrs. Baker can now struggle through a day in the classroom. She has managed this much progress through sheer perseverance and the help of a young daughter who has taken over the household chores. "My life right now revolves around work and rest." She spells it out: "There's no F-U-N!"

None of these Lake Tahoe regional residents described the kind of fatigue with which all of us are familiar. Few people who don't have it are able to imagine such deep and overwhelming prolonged weariness.

THE VARIOUS KINDS OF NORMAL FATIGUE

There are different forms of fatigue that all of us recognize:

Simple fatigue is either a mental or physical tiredness, following prolonged or intense activity. When someone engages in hard physical labor, the fatigue is usually muscular.

Everyone knows about simple muscle fatigue when insufficient rest fails to follow exertion. Muscle fatigue comes on because metabolic waste products accumulate in the muscles faster than they can be removed by the venous blood on its return passage to the lungs and heart. Rest and proper nourishment are the usual restoratives.

Deep tiredness or an overwhelming fatigue is a natural, normal diminution of energy when there are also great bodily changes taking place, such as during adolescence, pregnancy, breastfeeding, menopause, and in old age. A loss of vitality accompanied by non-response of body and mind to stimuli from the outside world will be present in extreme fatigue or exhaustion.

Emotional exhaustion—also called *psychasthenia*—is usually temporary, frequently occurring after people rally all their psychic forces to deal with some major crisis, such as a death in the family or the shock of a divorce. In a well person, such extreme fatigue can be gradually alleviated by getting enough sleep, returning to the routine of daily living, and planning congenial recreation.

Nervous fatigue is a symptom of emotional conflicts that cause anxiety. In the constant subconscious effort to find a satisfactory resolution to such conflicts, an enormous amount of psychic energy is expended, often to no purpose.

Another cause of fatigue is fear—commonly a fear of failure—which sometimes affects business executives as well as creative artists. Fatigue may strike as a subconscious means of avoiding some unpleasant task.

All these relatively simple forms of fatigue are manifested by a tendency to yawn, drowsiness, sweating, irritability, depression, general slowness of action, and forgetfulness. But none of these forms of simple fatigue can compare with the debilitating effects of chronic fatigue as manifested in the Downhill Syndrome.

HOW DOWNHILL SYNDROME FATIGUE DIFFERS FROM REGULAR FATIGUE

The fatigue manifested by the Downhill Syndrome is different from regular fatigue in nearly all respects. The primary symptom of the Downhill Syndrome fatigue is an inveterate depletion of energy, draining of strength, and total wearing out of a person to the point of absolute disability.

This fatigue arises unexpectedly, without any connection to intense physical activity, pregnancy, menopause, stress, or emotional conflicts. Rest and proper nourishment offer no respite. In addition, while normal fatigue usually disappears in a few days, the fatigue felt by victims of the Downhill Syndrome lasts at least six months and, in many cases, lasts years.

In addition to this debilitating fatigue, the Downhill Syndrome has other signs and symptoms, including:

- Abdominal pain
- Acute general body pain
- Alternating hot flushes and chills
- Anemia
- Bleeding of the gums, under the skin, and from mucous membranes
- Bloody phlegm
- Brown pigmentation
- Crying jags
- Dehydration and weight loss
- Diarrhea and cramps
- Difficulty walking
- Dizziness and fainting
- Double or blurred vision
- Enlarged lymph nodes
- Excessive urination and thirst
- Fingernails longitudinally ridged
- Foul-smelling phlegm
- Heartburn
- High blood pressure
- Impotence and loss of libido
- Incessant cough
- Inflammation of the joints
- Insomnia
- Jaundice

- Leg cramps
- Lethargy
- Loss of appetite
- Malnutrition
- Muscle weakness
- Nausea and vomiting
- Nervous and mental disorders
- Noises in the ear
- Nose bleeds
- Numbness and tingling
- Pain in bones
- Pale, waxy skin
- Periods of depression and anxiety
- Poor physical development
- Prostate trouble
- Pulsating headache in back of head
- Rapid heartbeat
- Shortness of breath
- Sore throat
- Sudden distaste for certain foods
- Swelling and fluid in the tissues
- Swollen genitalia
- Thrush
- Unexplained fever
- Vaginitis with discharge

Manifestations of the Downhill Syndrome can be constitutional (affecting the whole body) and pathognomonic (pointing to a particular body system, organ, tissue, or group of cells). There may be sympathetic symptoms in which discomfort is experienced in a part of the body other than the site of the disease. These characteristics can become well-established and persist for long periods. They involve slow changes, and their associated disabilities can be severe.

A REVISED DEFINITION OF CFIDS

In the United States, an illness is acknowledged only if the Centers for Disease Control and Prevention (CDC) define it as one. Coverage by private health insurance companies and the Social Security Administration is based on the CDC's official definition.

In 1994, the CDC revised their definition of CFIDS. By substantially reducing the number of symptoms a patient must display before receiving a confirmed diagnosis of CFIDS, the organization's revised definition makes it easier for doctors to arrive at a diagnosis and get on with treating the patient's discomforts.

According to the published revision, indications of a patient's CFIDS must include:

A. The new onset of fatigue that is causing a 50 percent reduction in one's activity for at least six months.

B. Exclusion of other illnesses that cause fatigue.

C. Eight of the following eleven signs and symptoms: [1] mild fever, [2] recurrent sore throat, [3] painful lymph nodes, [4] muscle weakness, [5] myalgia, [6] prolonged fatigue after mild exercise, [7] recurrent headache, [8] migratory arthralgia, [9] neuropsychological complaints, [10] sleep disturbance, and [11] sudden onset of the symptom complex.

An explanation of these criteria has been offered by Nelson M. Gantz, M.D., clinical professor of medicine at Pennsylvania State University College of Medicine, and chief of the division of infectious diseases at The Polyclinic Medical Center in Harrisburg, PA.

The first major criterion, A, is that the complaint must be a new onset of persistent or relapsing debilitating fatigue or easy fatigability in a person who has no previous history of similar symptoms. The patient's fatigability does not resolve with bed rest. In addition, the patient's condition is severe enough to reduce average daily activity to less than half the earlier level for at least six months.

The second major criterion, B, states that other clinical conditions possibly producing similar symptoms must be excluded by thorough evaluation, based on the patient's history, physical examination, and appropriate laboratory findings. Other conditions may be malignancy; autoimmune disease; localized infection, such as occult abscess; chronic or subacute bacterial disease, such as endocarditis, Lyme disease, or tuberculosis; fungal disease, such as histoplasmosis, blastomycosis, or coccidioidomycosis; parasitic disease, such as toxoplasmosis, amebiasis, giardiasis, or helminthic infestation; and disease related to the human immunodeficiency virus infection, such as AIDS or AIDS-related complex (ARC).

Chronic psychiatric disease, such as certain kinds of depression, hysterical personality disorder, anxiety neurosis, and schizophrenia must be considered as well. The habitual use of tranquilizers, lithium, or antidepressive medications strongly suggests the presence of chronic psychiatric disease.

Other possible diagnoses are chronic inflammatory disease, such as sarcoidosis, Wegener's granulomatosis, or chronic hepatitis; neuromuscular disease, such as multiple sclerosis or myasthenia gravis; and endocrine disease, such as hypothyroidism, Addison's disease, Cushing's syndrome, or diabetes mellitus.

Known or potential chronic pulmonary, cardiac, gastrointestinal, hepatic, renal, and hematologic disease must be ruled out. In addition, chemical causes must be considered, including drug dependency or abuse, and side effects of a chronic medication or another toxic agent, such as a chemical solvent, pesticide, or heavy metal.

Among the so-called minor criteria set by the CDC case definition are several references to symptoms C. A given symptom must have begun at or after the time of onset of increased fatigability and must have persisted or recurred for at least six months. Individual symptoms need not necessarily have occurred simultaneously.

The affirmed symptoms must include any eight of the following eleven:

1. Mild fever ranging between 100° F to 102° F (taken orally) or chills.

2. Sore throat (persistent pain and discomfort when swallowing).

3. Painful lymph nodes distributed in the front or back cervical region and under the armpits.

4. Unexplained generalized muscle weakness, so patient has difficulty performing normal daily activities.

5. Muscle discomfort or myalgia.

6. Generalized fatigue for twenty-four hours or more after exercising at a level that formerly would have been easily tolerated.

7. Generalized headaches of a type, severity, or pattern that is different from headaches the patient may have had before the onset of CFIDS.

8. Migratory arthralgia (in which pains switch from joint to joint) without the presence of joint swelling or redness.

9. Neuropsychological complaints, including an unreal fear of light (photophobia), temporary blind spots making their appearance in the visual field (transient visual scotomata), forgetfulness, excessive irritability, confusion, difficulty in thinking, inability to concentrate, or depression.

10. Sleep disturbance, including excessively long sleep periods (hypersomnia) or the inability to sleep (insomnia).

11. A description of the main symptom complex as initially developing over a few hours to a few days. (This is not a true symptom, but is considered valid for meeting the CDC case definition).

Dr. Gantz explains that although specific laboratory tests and clinical measurements are not required to satisfy the CDC case definition of CFIDS, there is a recommended evaluation that includes:

• Monthly weight measurements, with a weight change of more than 10 percent in the absence of dieting, suggesting other diagnoses.

• Daily morning and afternoon temperatures monitored for one to two weeks.

• A complete blood count and differential reading; the laboratory blood testing for serum electrolytes, glucose, creatinine, blood urea nitrogen, calcium, phosphorus, total bilirubin, alkaline phosphatase, serum aspartate aminotransferase, serum alanine aminotransferase, creatinine phosphokinase or aldolase; urinalysis; and an erythrocyte sedimentation rate.

• An antinuclear antibody test, thyroid-stimulating hormone level, HIV antibody measurement, and intermediate-strength purified protein derivative (PPD) skin test with controls.

• Posteroanterior and lateral chest X-ray films.

• Detailed personal and family psychiatric history.

Abnormal test findings prompt a search for other conditions that may cause such results. If no other conditions are detected by a reasonable evaluation, this criterion for a diagnosis of the Downhill Syndrome is satisfied.

And, as we will see, there are a variety of other physical problems that may act not as causes of the disease, but as cofactors, prolonging and deepening its symptoms.

3.

SEARCHING FOR THE CAUSES OF THE DOWNHILL SYNDROME

When the body is in a constant state of good health, it is defined in medicine as *homeostasis*. If one's balance between opposing bodily functions and the chemical compositions of fluids and tissues remains in place, the body is not susceptible to pathology. Keeping your body in homeostasis is, therefore, the source of ongoing wellness.

HOW HOMEOSTASIS IS ALTERED

A key concept for understanding the chronic fatigue and associated symptoms of the Downhill Syndrome is body system balance. To sustain life, water, nutrients, sunlight, and numerous other elements must be present, but they don't have to be ideal in quantity. The required life-sustaining elements merely must be adequate.

Because the body has a reserve capacity, it can adjust even if outside invaders such as viruses are thrown into its terrain. Only when the body's balance between internal and external environments is upset in the extreme will it be unable to bounce back and thrive. When the body's homeostasis is upset and the body becomes weakened, scavenging pests find a comfortable place to reside and prosper. The pests could be Epstein-Barr virus (EBV), cytomegalovirus, *Candida albicans*, herpes simplex I or II, human herpesvirus-VI, other viruses, parasites, bacteria, metallic poisons, or something equally destructive. From the basis of research so far, these are the main culprits responsible for the Downhill Syndrome.

The term "culprits," however, is a rather simplistic one that has two important and specific meanings: 1. A cause, or a causative factor, and 2. A cofactor, or a contributing factor. A cause, sometimes referred to as an "agent," is a single factor that causes a disease or syndrome. For example, a bacteria known as B-hemolytic streptococcus A is a cause of strept throat, and the EBV is a cause of infectious mononucleosis. No other bacteria causes strept throat, and no other virus causes infectious mononucleosis.

A cofactor does not cause a disease or condition, but makes it easier for a cause to do its work. For example, in the case of infectious mononucleosis, where EBV is a cause, a cytomegalovirus may play the role of cofactor by putting extra strain on the immune system.

The Downhill Syndrome has, as yet, no known cause. The National Institute of Allergy and Infectious Diseases (NIAID) advisory subcommittee states: "Given that a single etiology [for CFIDS] has not been found, it is important that investigators continue to think of it as a symptom-complex and not a single disease and thus allow themselves to consider multiple etiologies." Therefore, all the suspected agents in this book fit the category of a "cofactor."

What factors might upset the balance in the body and alter homeostasis? Lots of actions in our daily lives do it. Here is a listing of fifteen factors that potentially weaken people's immune systems when frequently repeated:

1. Eating too much processed food, including ice cream, trans fat-fried potatoes, fatty hamburgers, and Danish pastries.

2. Undergoing psychological stress.

3. Ingesting chemical additives and artificial coloring agents.

4. Absorbing mercury gas particules into the body, caused by chewing on amalgam fillings lodged in dental cavities.

5. Absorbing various pollutants present in the air and water.

6. Exposing the body to radiation from such products as microwave ovens, X-ray equipment, and radiation treatment for cancer and other malignancies.

7. Overmedicating as part of a routine health maintenance program or for recreational purposes.

8. Habitually drinking alcohol, including whiskey, beer,

wine, and other alcoholic beverages.

9. Smoking or chewing tobacco.

10. Consuming rancid fats, such as those found in spoiled salad dressings.

11. Eating vegetables and fruits grown in nutrient-exhausted soils.

12. Taking too high dosages of megavitamins or megaminerals.

13. Ingesting inorganic minerals rather than organic ones.

14. Absorbing toxic agents such as pesticides and insecticides.

15. Exposing the body to free radicals emitted by video display terminals.

The populations of industrialized nations are suffering from medically incurable viral conditions at alarmingly increasing rates. More bacterial infections are becoming resistant to commonly used antibiotics. Secondary immune disorders, like the thrush of *Candida albicans,* are becoming more prevalent. All of these types of health problems reflect the declining capacity of the human immune system, a decline caused by the very advancements sought after by modern man.

OUR TECHNOLOGICAL IMPROVEMENTS ARE KILLING US

The human body is being forced to cope with an environment it has never before experienced. According to John Bennett, M.D., Assistant Director of the Center for Infectious Diseases, National Centers for Disease Control and Prevention in Atlanta, Georgia: "Organisms have found new ways of getting to us, mostly through mankind's own advances."

Technological improvements as diverse as hot air ducts, air conditioning, airplane passenger cabins, food processing, hair sprays, antibiotics, the birth control pill, and tampons, among thousands of other items, have created ideal breeding grounds for germs that have been dormant for millennia. Modern transportation has brought exotic microorganisms to populations on opposite sides of the world.

This altered environment has caused people's immune systems to weaken, leaving them vulnerable to new and devastating infections. The normal immune system is our personal legacy from millions of years of evolution. It is a multi-part, many-tiered, incredibly sophisticated system by which one's body is able to naturally resist disease and infection. But we are damaging ourselves immunologically by means of mankind's natural affinity to high technology and synthetic living.

The Downhill Syndrome is a unique outgrowth of the loss of nature from our surroundings—forcing all of us to adapt to synthetic external influences. Survival is the issue, because some people find it impossible to adapt.

THE POSSIBLE CONNECTION OF MICROFLORAS AND THE DOWNHILL SYNDROME

An additional theory about the cause of the Downhill Syndrome focuses on the role of microorganisms in the body and how they can be altered by internal and external conditions. Some microorganisms take on multiple forms during their life cycles. Certain microorganisms in the form of microflora—bacteria, viruses, parasites, and fungi—have the unique characteristic of being able to change from one form to another, depending on conditions inside the body. The scientific theory on which this concept is formed was given by the early twentieth-century German bacteriologist Guenther Enderlein. Dr. Enderlein took his cue from the nineteenth-century French microbiologist Antoine Bechamp, whose original concept was called *pleomorphism.*

Pleomorphism is the change of any living organism into a number of different protoplasmic shapes, forms, or other identifying characteristics during its life cycle. Examples of pleomorphic forms in nature include the caterpillar's emergence into a butterfly and the tadpole into a frog. Although conventional medicine has ignored pleomorphism's role in disease, Dr. Enderlein spent nearly six decades studying it.

As medical journalist Michael Sheehan explains: "According to the German researcher [Dr. Enderlein], some microbial forms that live in human blood and body fluids are, under certain conditions, associated with many of the worst chronic diseases known to humankind. He asserted that when a person is healthy, these microbes are helpful to the body's immune system and live with the other cells in a symbiotic relationship. Any severe change or deterioration of the body's internal environment, however—as when the pH value of the blood and fluids become acidic or alkaline due to poor nutrition, smoking, or other factors—could cause the microbes to change into disease-causing forms as they pass through specific stages of their life cycle."

Some researchers believe that everyday toxins may cause pleomorphism of the body's microflora, and that this change may be a cause of the Downhill Syndrome.

How Pleomorphism Created A Deadly Virus

An example of the potentially harmful effects of pleomorphism involves a virus normally found in humans, that had been demonstrated as harmless to mice. When laboratory mice were made to suffer from a nutritional deficiency, however, the virus spontaneously changed and caused heart damage. Once changed, the investigating scientists said, the virus was also able to infect and damage the hearts of nutritionally well-balanced mice. In other words, this virus had turned into a pleomorphic form and become deadly. The researchers added that nutritional inadequacies in humans may also aid viral mutation, which conforms to the concept of pleomorphism.

The researchers, headed by Melinda A. Beck, Ph.D., of the University of North Carolina at Chapel Hill, chose to study the coxsackie virus, a type of virus with the genetic core of ribonucleic acid (RNA) instead of deoxyribonucleic acid (DNA).

As mentioned earlier, viruses with their genetic code written in RNA are known to sustain many mutations when they reproduce, because they do not have a corrective mechanism for recognizing and repairing replication errors, as do DNA viruses.

How Researchers Induced the Viral Change

Dr. Beck and her colleagues fed one group of mice a normal diet and fed another group food that was deficient in the trace nutrient selenium. After four weeks, both groups were exposed to a type of cox-sackie virus called B3 that is normally harmless to mice. The virus had no effect on the mice fed normal diets, but severely damaged the hearts of those on selenium-deficient diets in seven to ten days.

After recovering samples of the virus from selenium-deficient mice, the scientists transferred this virus to healthy mice on normal diets. The mice also developed significant heart damage, suggesting that the virus had mutated into a virulent form that could attack even mice receiving sufficient selenium. The scientists said they repeated the experiment three months later and got the same results.

Interpreting the Findings

Speculating on why the selenium deficiency affected mutation of the virus, the researchers said it was possible that the deficient mice had weaker immune responses, which allowed the coxsackie virus to multiply faster and produce more genetic errors; another possi-bility was that selenium is an antioxidant, which protects genes from the damaging effects of certain types of oxygen in the body that act as free radicals (agents that can damage body cells and tis-sues).

The researchers also said that the findings highlighted a little-suspected mechanism for viruses to change and become more path-ogenic. If the nutritional status of the infected host proves to affect other disease-causing viruses of the type studied, Dr. Beck said, it may turn out to be a factor in the evolution of more deadly forms of influenza, hepatitis, meningitis, and other illnesses affecting humans, such as the Downhill Syndrome.

Most adults in the United States are immune to coxsackie virus-es (there are twenty-nine known types) because they were infected while young and developed antibodies to them. Although coxsack-ie infections generally are not severe, producing a range of symp-toms including sore throats, colds, aches, and inflammation, in about 10 percent of cases, people do suffer severe disease symp-toms. These symptoms include inflammation of the layer sur-rounding the heart muscle (pericarditis) or inflammation and infec-tion of the brain (meningitis).

Dr. Beck's group of scientists studied coxsackie B3 virus because it has been linked to a heart condition known as Keshan disease.

Once common in China among children and women of childbearing age living in selenium-deficient areas, Keshan disease has been mostly eradicated in that country by widespread use of dietary supplements that include selenium.

HOW NUTRITION CONNECTS WITH
THE DOWNHILL SYNDROME

Investigators in the United Kingdom are studying the connection between enteroviruses (the same family of virus that caused poliomyelitis), particularly human coxsackie B virus, and the Downhill Syndrome. One study of ninety-six patients found enteroviral RNA in muscle biopsies of about 21 percent of those who had CFIDS, compared with none in a control group. Yet, at the Pennsylvania State University College of Medicine, clinical professor of medicine Nelson M. Gantz, M.D., and his colleagues were unable to identify coxsackie antibody in the blood of twenty patients with the Downhill Syndrome, and all stool cultures were negative for enteroviruses.

Still other researchers are trying to understand the connection between dietary differences, pleomorphism, and the Downhill Syndrome. For example, Charles Gauntt, M.D., of the University of Texas Health Science Center, and Steve Tracy, M.D., of the University of Nebraska Medical Center, noted that dietary deficiencies had a role in other viral problems. They cited, for example, that treating a vitamin A deficiency among children in developing countries had reduced the severity of measles.

The two university physicians said many questions remained, including determining whether periodic or minor nutritive deficiencies, not just major ones as in the Beck study, encourage development of deadlier viruses or exacerbate human viral infections. "Perhaps virus evolution does depend on what we eat or what we do not eat," they stated. That is as close a connection as those researchers are now willing to make.

The authors of this book take a more definitive stand. After considering the evidence, we believe that a person's nutritional status can determine when and how the symptoms of the Downhill Syndrome will develop.

4.

DIAGNOSING THE DOWNHILL SYNDROME

Since the initial outbreaks of CFIDS, a dedicated group of physicians and researchers has explored both the causes and effects of this disease. Research into the effects of CFIDS on the immune response has made great progress. It is now possible to study immune defense system cells on an individual basis. Examination of white blood cell subsets, for example, has shown distinct differences in certain lymphocytes (types of white blood cells that perform immune functions) between CFIDS patients and healthy individuals. Researchers have also found changes in the levels of certain serum proteins in patients with the Downhill Syndrome.

DIAGNOSTIC TESTS FOR THE DOWNHILL SYNDROME

By zeroing in on such differences, researchers have come up with many highly sophisticated tests that are now available to the CFIDS patient community through primary-care physicians. As with any disease state, no single test can accurately diagnose such a complex illness as the Downhill Syndrome. To make a diagnosis of CFIDS, doctors must perform an overall laboratory evaluation of the immune system.

Today, there is real hope not only of establishing more accurate criteria for making a diagnosis, but also for monitoring how the immune system responds during therapy. Many analytical labs offer the tests we are about to describe. The information about these tests and their proposed pricing has been provided by Oncore

Analytics, a clinical laboratory located at 4900 Fannin, Houston, Texas 77004 U.S.A.; telephone (800) 662-6738 or (713) 523-6100; FAX (713) 523-8528. The following lab tests have been found useful in diagnosing the Downhill Syndrome:

- *Mitogen-Activated Lymphocytes (MALIBU) Test:* Mitogens are substances that bring about cellular subdivision (mitosis). The lymphocytes of a healthy person will respond vigorously to mitogen activation. For instance, such activation stimulates the lymphocytes to produce lymphokines, which in turn cause the cells to begin protein and DNA synthesis, necessary for the creation of new lymphocytes. In contrast, the lymphocytes of an AIDS or CFIDS patient frequently do not respond in such a way to mitogen stimulation. When physicians see this lack of response, they diagnose a state of immunosuppression, the state in which antibodies are inactive, allowing substances to invade the body.

The MALIBU technique evaluates lymphocytes on a cell-by-cell basis, providing a clear picture of the response of each cell to the particular mitogen. The proposed physician cost of the MALIBU test is $150.

- *Human Herpesvirus DNA Detection Assays:* The Human Herpesviruses (HHV) are known to cause immunosuppression and disease in humans. Herpesviruses can also cause retroviruses such as HIV to intensify disease. There are three classes of Herpesviruses implicated in the cause of CFIDS:

1. The Epstein-Barr Virus (EBV) was originally thought to be the prime cause of the Downhill Syndrome, since it is known to be the source of infectious mononucleosis. In addition, CFIDS was once thought to be produced by a chronic EBV infection. Although we now know this is not always true, EBV has been detected in many patients with CFIDS.

2. While infection with Cytomegalovirus (CMV) usually produces more severe symptomatology than that shown in CFIDS, CMV has been detected in patients with the Downhill Syndrome.

3. Human Herpesvirus Type VI (HHV-VI) has also been found in patients with CFIDS.

Detection of these three human Herpesviruses is now possible using sophisticated viral culture techniques combined with molecular biology. Active infection with EBV, CMV, or HHV-VI may now be uncovered using the DNA Detection Assay.

The proposed physician cost of the Human Herpesvirus DNA Detection Assay for each of the tests to detect EBV, CMV, or HHV-VI is $150.

- *EBV, CMV, and HHV-VI Antibody Titers:* Although the previous tests are more sensitive, physicians routinely ask clinical laboratories to perform antibody blood titer testing for the human Herpesviruses implicated in the Downhill Syndrome. A titer is the volume of a substance or microorganism in the test solution, in this case, blood. Levels of IgG and IgM antibodies in the blood are reported.

The proposed physician cost of the EBV Antibody blood titer test is $80; the CMV Antibody blood titer test is $40; the HHV-VI Antibody blood titer test is $75.

- *Natural Killer Cell Cytotoxicity Assay:* Natural Killer cells (NK cells) are a subset of lymphocytes normally found in the blood. The NK cell is thought to act as a first line of defense against abnormal cells: cells that are damaged, precancerous or cancerous, or virally infected. In patients with the Downhill Syndrome, low NK cell activity has been observed. As we mentioned earlier, in Japan, CFIDS is referred to as Low Natural Killer Cell Activity Syndrome. The proposed physician cost of this NK test is $175.

- *Lymphocyte Enumeration Panel:* Counting T and B cell lymphocyte subsets using the technique of flow cytometry is an accepted determination of a patient's immune status. Any combination of white blood cell subsets may be analyzed using flow cytometry.

The following markers are included by most labs: the Total T cells (CD_2), the Helper T cells (CD_4), the Suppressor T cells (CD_8), the Total B cells (CD_{20}), and the CD_4/CD_8 ratio. Each value is given a relative percentage and absolute number by the testing laboratory. A high number of the Helper T cells indicates an active state of the immune system; a high count of the Suppressor T cells signals that extreme activity of the Helper T cells is no longer needed and, therefore, Suppressor T cells are being called to slow the Helper T cells down. A CD_4/CD_8 ratio of lower than 0.6:1.0 indicates a state of immunosuppression. The proposed physician cost of this lymphocyte enumeration test is $80.

- *Lymphocyte Immune Dysfunction Panel:* To more completely evaluate the lymphocyte subsets of a given patient blood sample, clinical labs often suggest the following panel: the Total T cells (CD_2), the Helper T cells (CD_4), the Suppressor T cells (CD_8), the Monocytes, LGLs, C3bi receptor (CD_{11b}), the Total B cells (CD_{20}), the Thymocytes, activated T cells (CD_{38}), the Natural Killer cells (CD_{56}), the B cell light-chain markers (Kappa, Lambda), the class II HLA marker (HLA-Dr), and the CD_4/CD_8 ratio. Each value is given a relative percentage and absolute number by the testing lab. Low counts of Total T cells and Helper T cells point to immunosuppression. The proposed physician cost of this lymphocyte dysfunction test is $195.

- *Interleukin-2 Serum Level:* Interleukin-2 (IL-2) is responsible for the propagation, expansion, and activation of T cells. IL-2 also stimulates NK cells and Lymphocyte Activated Killer cells (LAK cells) to carry out their protective functions. Certain immunosuppressive diseases, such as AIDS, cause a decrease in circulating serum levels of IL-2; other diseases that affect the immune system, such as multiple sclerosis, systemic lupus erythematosis, and CFIDS, cause an increase in serum levels. Infection with CMV has also been demonstrated to cause an elevated serum level of IL-2. The proposed physician cost of this IL-2 blood test is $50.

- *Soluble Interleukin-2 Receptor Level (sIL-2R):* The IL-2 receptor is normally located on the surface of T cell lymphocytes. Its role is to bind circulating IL-2, causing expansion of the T cell population. During T cell activation, a certain amount of IL-2 receptor is shed into the serum. High serum levels of this receptor have been found in patients with autoimmune diseases such as lupus, viral infections such as EBV and HIV, and in a variety of leukemias and lymphomas. Elevated levels of sIL-2R have been demonstrated in greater than 50 percent of patients with the Downhill Syndrome. The proposed physician cost of this test is $50.

- *Interleukin-6 (IL-6) Serum Level:* Interleukin-6 (IL-6) is a multifunctional lymphokine essential to normal immune system function. IL-6 helps induce B cell differentiation and stimulates IgG secretion. IL-6 is secreted by a number of cell types including fibroblasts, monocytes, endothelial cells, and activated T cells. Low levels of IL-6 point to immunosuppression, and have been detected in CFIDS patients. The proposed physician cost of this IL-6 blood test is $50.

- *Soluble CD-8 Receptor Level (sCD-8R):* The receptor on certain cells known as suppressors, designated CD-8R, is shed into the serum of patients when T suppressor/cytotoxic lymphocytes are activated. More than 50 percent of Downhill Syndrome patients have elevated levels of the soluble CD-8R. The proposed physician cost of this CD-8 receptor test is $50.

- *Soluble CD-23 Receptor Level (sCD-23R):* The CD-23 molecule is normally found on the surface of lymphocytes and macrophages, the immune system's large scavenger cells that engulf and digest bacteria, viruses, fungi, and cancer cells, among other cellular debris. Certain inflammatory diseases, such as rheumatoid arthritis, have been associated with abnormally high levels of sCD-23R. Since B cell function is often impaired in Downhill Syndrome patients, measuring the serum level of sCD-23R may be a useful indicator of disease progression. The proposed physician cost of this CD-23 receptor test is $50.

- *Alpha-Interferon Serum Level:* Alpha-Interferon (IFN-alpha) is produced by lymphocytes in response to a virus. Increases in circulating levels of IFN-alpha can cause fatigue, malaise, and low-grade fever, all common symptoms of Downhill Syndrome patients. Indeed, many of the patients having this disease show increased levels of IFN-alpha. The proposed physician cost of this alpha-interferon test is $75.

- *Chronic Fatigue Associated Retrovirus Assay (CARA):* In 1991, Elaine DeFreitas, Ph.D., and her colleagues at the Wistar Institute in Philadelphia reported that a large percentage of Downhill Syndrome patients had a retroviral sequence in the DNA that suggests the presence of the virus HTLV-II. The CARA tests for this "virus-like" sequence. A positive result indicates that the same specific DNA sequence detected by Dr. DeFreitas is present. The exact meaning of such a finding, and the relationship of this sequence to CFIDS, is still not understood, but it implicates a viral cause for the disease. The proposed physician cost of this retrovirus test is $150.

• *IgG Subclasses Serum Level:* Deficiencies in one or more of the four IgG subclasses have been associated with recurrent respiratory tract infections, recurrent bacteremia (presence of bacteria in the blood), unusual allergies, and an immunodeficient response to certain antigens in bacteria. These are all symptoms that often show up in CFIDS patients. The proposed physician cost of this IgG blood test is $75.

This group of highly sophisticated tests allows physicians to obtain additional information concerning the condition of their patients' immune systems. This information is even more valuable if you consider the absence of any universal test that would indisputably determine the presence of CFIDS. If routine tests fail to pinpoint the cause of their symptoms, patients should request these tests to aid in diagnosing the Downhill Syndrome.

5

Metabolic Immunodepression

Metabolism is the basic chemical and physical process that continuously goes on in organisms and cells. When a person's metabolism does not function properly, the body is thrown into a non-homeostatic position. This simplified version of a very complex process explains why diabetic patients are more predisposed to getting bacterial and fungal infections than healthy people, why pregnant women frequently come down with yeast infections, and why the elderly catch colds more easily and recover from them more slowly than do younger people. In patients suffering from CFIDS, a malfunctioning metabolism also negatively affects their immune status, causing metabolic immunodepression, or MID, the main source of almost all the signs and symptoms of the Downhill Syndrome.

The term immunity refers to all mechanisms used by the body as protection against substances that are foreign to it. A broad definition of immunology is the mechanism by which the body distinguishes what is "self" from what is "non-self." Scientist Paul Yanick, Jr., Ph.D., director of the Center for Biological Energetics in Milford, Pennsylvania, offers a clear overview of the five main tasks of the immune system.

DEFINING A HEALTHY IMMUNE SYSTEM

Dr. Yanick's list of the immune system's five tasks includes:

1. Defense—defeating and eliminating microorganisms and toxins.

2. Homeostasis—self-cleansing and balancing with other systems.

3. Surveillance—building up of antibodies and immunologic memory.

4. Repair—rebuilding of damaged or "weakened" organs and glands.

5. Boundaries—maintaining boundaries with the environment.

People are constantly fighting imperceptable wars against toxins, invading microbes and other foreign invaders. We rely on the help of different organs, tissues, cells, fluids, and molecules—components of our immune defense system—to act as a sort of collective second brain to counteract the invaders. If one or more of these components is impaired, your immune system is said to dysfunction.

A DESCRIPTION OF METABOLIC IMMUNODEPRESSION

Metabolic immunodepression is caused by a disturbance in carbohydrate or lipid metabolism. To understand the complex physiological mechanisms involving MID, let's see what happens when someone ingests two grams of sugar (glucose) present in a piece of cake. In a healthy person, the two grams of glucose are used without difficulty, stored in the body until they are converted into fuel to be burned in the production of metabolic energy.

But suppose those two grams of glucose are ingested by an out-of-shape adult who is overweight, underexercised, occupationally stressed, facing a divorce, smoking two packs of cigarettes daily, drinking three cups of coffee for breakfast, using recreational street drugs in the evening, eating fast foods for lunch, and otherwise nutritionally malnourished. Then, those glucose grams end up becoming almost lethal additions to the diet.

What happens is that the hypothalamus isn't able to burn both grams. The hypothalamus is a portion of the brain that activates, controls, and integrates part of the endocrine processes, nervous system, and many bodily functions, such as temperature, sleep, and appetite. It may take up, store, and finally burn off only one glucose gram as a fuel source. What happens to the second gram? It sets off the following unhealthy chain reaction inside the body:

- It leaves the gastrointestinal tract and enters the bloodstream, causing hyperglycemia, a jump in the blood's glucose level.

- The increase in blood glucose triggers the pancreas to dump insulin into the bloodstream, creating a condition known as hyperinsulinemia.

- This condition, in turn, causes two others: 1) an opposite reaction known as hypoglycemia, in which the blood's glucose level is lowered, and 2) a triggering of the growth hormone to remove fat from its deposits for more energy, increasing the number of free fatty acids.

- Elevated blood levels of free fatty acids force the liver to work harder, so it produces an increased blood level of low-density lipoprotein (LDL) cholesterol. As we know, an elevated level of LDL is a source of atherosclerotic plaque. In addition, with an excess, cellular plasma membranes that are usually flexible so the cells can change shape and fluidity become rigid and inflexible.

This chain reaction, illustrated in Figure 5.1 (on next page), occurs in all cells of the body, including the primary cells of the immune system, the lymphocytes. Ordinarily, the healthy immune system produces lymphocytes, a process known as lymphocytic blastogenesis. This process produces hundreds of thousands of T-lymphocytes and millions of other white blood cells that act as an immune system army to conquer invasions of pathogenic microorganisms. When lymphocytic plasma membrane becomes rigid, a decrease in the growth factors Interleukin-1 and Interleukin-2 occurs. In turn, without enough stimulation by these growth factors, the number of new lymphocytes declines. And, with a shortage of lymphocytes, the immune system cannot function at full capacity, which brings the lowering of cellular immunity known as MID.

At a 1992 meeting of the American College for Advancement in Medicine, Dr. Yutsis demonstrated that a majority of Downhill patients show the presence of one to four major parameters of MID. In fact, 76 percent of the patients revealed three paramaters of MID. This points to MID as a major contributor to the development of the Downhill Syndrome.

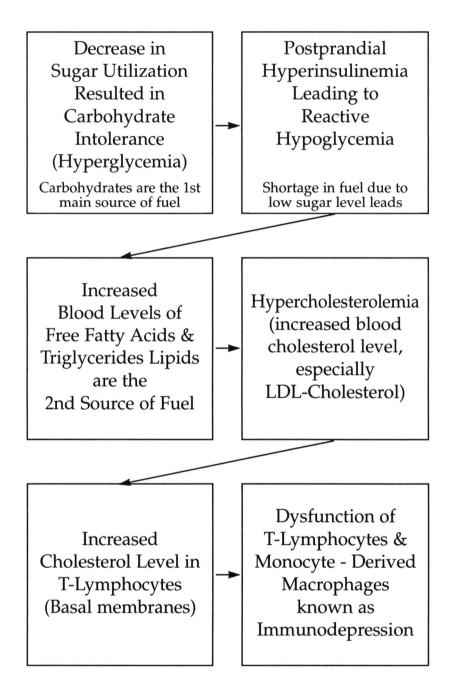

Figure 5.1: The Model of Metabolic Immunodepression

THE FOUR MAJOR PARAMETERS OF MID

MID is characterized by four major parameters, identified almost twenty-five years ago by Russian research physician Vladimir Dilman, but only now being accepted into American medicine as true disease categories. Professor Dilman found that disturbances of carbohydrate and lipid metabolism bring dysfunction of the macrophages (large scavenger cells), among other blood elements. As his former "resident-in-training," Dr. Yutsis studied these ideas and added clinical research of his own.

The four major parameters are:

1. An intolerance to the ingestion of refined sugar in nearly any form. The patient develops signs and symptoms of disease from a so-called "carbohydrate intolerance."

2. An overabundant amount of insulin permeating the blood following a meal, especially if sugar is a part of that meal.

3. A general elevation in the blood's free-fatty-acid level.

4. An increase in the LDL level of the blood.

This last factor is associated with an accumulation of cholesterol in the plasma membranes of the immune defense blood elements, in particular the vital double-defense components of the T-lymphocytes and those large scavenger cells called macrophages.

In MID, there is usually a reduction in the ability of the macrophages to engulf and digest bacteria, viruses, fungi, cancer cells, protozoa, and other cellular debris. In other words, while the macrophages have the designated purpose of gobbling up foreign particles, in a person with MID, macrophages fail to do their immunological job.

If even one of these four MID parameters is present in a patient, the individual will likely experience some suppression of the immune system. When all four of these parameters are present, the individual is in a state of severely depressed immunity—the same state for anyone exhibiting symptoms of the Downhill Syndrome.

A MID PATIENT

In April, 1989, twenty-two-year-old Laura Ann Maloney of

Bridgewater, New Jersey, a file clerk employed by a major bank, sought diagnosis and corrective treatment for a variety of health troubles from Dr. Yutsis. She suffered from severe fatigue, diarrhea, vaginal discharge, abdominal cramping, nausea, vomiting, heartburn, chest pains, chronic throat irritation, frequent sore throats, repeated fits of coughing, and light-headedness. In addition, she suffered from confusion, spaciness, disorientation, and the inability to retain thoughts even for a few seconds.

Seven other physicians practicing conventional medicine could not diagnose the source of Laura's health problems. They suggested that she consult a psychiatrist, and one of them declared, "It's all in your head!"

It turns out, however, that Laura was following the typical pattern of discomforting symptoms and signs experienced by vast numbers of patients who suffer from MID. After undergoing some of the procedures discussed in Chapter Four, Laura was finally diagnosed.

Diagnostic blood, urine, and other lab tests showed that Laura suffered from a very low white blood-cell count, EBV, and multiple allergies to photocopier ink, printer ribbons, cigarette smoke, and chemicals released from a newly installed office carpet. In addition, a blood test revealed abnormal blood levels that indicated chronic hypoglycemia, elevated triglycerides, and high LDL levels, and other tests pointed to a gastrointestinal and vaginal invasion of *Candida albicans,* or yeast.

In short, these test readings and subsequent diagnostic tests showed that Laura Mahoney was suffering from MID. As you'll see, Dr. Yutsis's treatment plan reversed the MID.

REVERSING MID

"Metabolic immunodepression may be mitigated and even eliminated by a pharmacologic correction of the [patient's] metabolic pattern," declared Russian Professor Vladimir Dilman during the course of his medical investigations in the early 1970s.

After much experimentation, the professor approached his correction of MID by altering the amount of the naturally occurring hormone insulin in his ill patients.

HOW INSULIN WORKS

Insulin is released by the pancreas in response to increased levels of sugar in the blood. It regulates the metabolism of sugar and some of the processes necessary for the metabolism of fats, carbohydrates, and proteins, lowers blood sugar levels, and promotes the transport and entry of sugar into the muscle cells and other tissues.

Many drugs interact with insulin, including the monoamine oxidase inhibitors, corticosteroids, salicylates, thiazide diuretics, and phenytoin. Fever, stress, infection, pregnancy, surgery, and hyperthyroidism may significantly increase insulin requirements, while liver disease, hypothyroidism, vomiting, and kidney disease may decrease them.

AN INSULIN EXPERIMENT

Dr. Dilman selected two groups of patients of different MID parameters for testing. The first group included women who were victims of breast cancer who showed symptoms of glucose intolerance, high blood insulin levels, elevation of LDL cholesterol levels, high triglyceride levels, high serum cholesterol levels, and low levels of new lymphocytes, suggesting immune depression.

The second group to be examined consisted of patients with ischemic heart disease (IHD), a condition characterized by episodes of diminished blood supply to the heart. It was logical to choose such heart- and blood-vessel-impaired patients because they obviously would be suffering from increased cholesterol and high triglyceride blood levels. Dr. Dilman discovered that a majority of the IHD patients also possessed elevated blood insulin levels, along with other abnormal parameters of MID.

How An Insulin-Reducing Drug Worked

Dr. Dilman placed both patient groups on an insulin-lowering, antidiabetic drug known as *phenformin,* and evaluated them at intervals of three, six, and nine months. What he found was that all of the abnormal parameters of MID were reversed. The patients' reproduction of lymphocytes was normalized. Merely by regulating the insulin levels of his patients, he had restored their immune systems, giving them back their ability to fend off foreign invaders.

Why Insulin Regulation Works

Researchers have looked for clues as to why insulin regulation works to correct MID. One 1972 study published in the *Journal of Clinical Endocrinology* suggested that another drug, phenytoin (commonly known as *Dilantin* ™), in addition to its anti-seizure action, dramatically diminished the release of glucagon. Glucagon, a hormone produced in the pancreas, changes glycogen to glucose in the liver, and is stimulated by a lowering of the blood sugar to correct hypoglycemia. So if phenytoin lowers the amount of glucagon, it lowers blood sugar levels, thereby producing an insulin-like effect. Another study in 1985 indicated that phenytoin has significant cholesterol and triglyceride-lowering effects.

The conclusion from these various studies is that the use of phenytoin improves three metabolic parameters of MID: insulin levels, triglyceride levels, and cholesterol levels. It is possible to conclude, therefore, that phenytoin can and does reverse MID. It would be reasonable to assume that if both phenformin and phenytoin can reverse MID, and MID is one of the main contributors to the development of CFIDS, then these drugs can cure CFIDS as well. Unfortunately, as we will see in later chapters, there are too many other underlying causes of the Downhill Syndrome for just one drug to cure it.

HOW FISH OILS CAN HELP ELIMINATE MID

Among other treatments, fish oils have been found to counteract the effects of MID. The benefits of adding fish oils to an intravenous blood flow has been reported by Jeffrey Askanazi, M.D., an associate professor leading a research group in the Department of Anesthesiology at the Mt. Sinai Medical Center in New York City. Dr. Askanazi's group used intravenous infusions of fish oils to treat inflammatory bowel disease. The researchers were able to improve their patients' condition and reverse the effects of MID.

The fish oil, containing Omega-3 fatty acids, brought about the following improvements:

- An increase in the number of lymphocytes in the patients.

- An improvement of cell-mediated immune responses.

- A decrease of triglyceride levels in blood plasma, as well as a decrease in LDL-cholesterol levels and an increase in HDL levels.

By analyzing Dr. Askanazi's research, and comparing it to the investigations of doctors in four other studies, we conclude that the omega-3 fatty acids in fish oil reversed three parameters of MID: triglyceride levels, LDL-cholesterol levels, and the functional abilities of lymphocytes and macrophages.

AN EFFECTIVE DRUG TREATMENT

Carol Jessop, M.D., an internist with the Fairmount Internal Medicine Group and Assistant Clinical Professor of Medicine at the University of California at San Francisco, followed 1,100 patients who exhibited symptoms of the Downhill Syndrome and MID.

Of Dr. Jessop's patients, 90 percent showed elevated LDL levels, which, as we've seen, represents one of the MID parameters. Symptoms of fatigue were so severe for these patients that Dr. Jessop declared, "Their separate illnesses would be more aptly called 'chronic devastation syndrome.'"

Dr. Jessop treated 900 of these patients with ketoconazole, a drug used to reverse symptoms of candidiasis (yeast infection), and placed them on a sugar-free diet. In just one year of this treatment, 529 patients reversed their MID, and another 232 had shown marked improvement. A yeast-free diet was shown to be instrumental in the regulation of the first parameter of MID. An intolerance to the digestion of refined sugars and a carbohydrate intolerance in a majority of patients was eliminated, leading to a decrease in their LDL levels.

Several wholistic physicians treating CFIDS patients have reported similar experiences. In his treatment of 100 patients with severe fatigue and elevated LDL levels, for example, Dr. Yutsis found that by offering a comprehensive program that included a sugar-free diet, MID was reversed in 86 percent of the patients.

A MULTI-LEVEL APPROACH TO COUNTERACTING MID

By the end of 1993, Jane Guiltinan, N.D., a clinical associate professor in the Natural Health Clinic at Bastyr College of Naturopathy in Seattle, Washington, had treated over 2,000 patients with MID by using a multi-level approach. As she explains:

"We attack what Dr. Yutsis has so astutely labeled the Downhill Syndrome on a number of fronts. First, we have patients clean up their diets, eliminating processed foods and excess sugar and animal fats, all of which predispose one to being affected by this ubiquitous metabolic immunodepression. We supplement their diets with multivitamins, plus extra oral and/or intravenous doses of vitamin C and beta-carotene. We use various herbs, too. Such herbal remedies can consist of *Hypericum perforatum* (St. John's wort), *Glycyrrhiza glabra* (licorice root), and *silybum marianum*, which all possess immune-enhancing properties."

Dr. Guiltinan also treats the liver. "Food and environmental allergies invariably damage Downhill Syndrome patients' immune systems, so detoxifying their livers is vital," she explains. "We additionally have patients eliminate all known allergens, limit their exposure to external chemicals, and get them to avoid toxic metals and heavy metals."

SIX GENERAL TREATMENT STEPS FOR
ELIMINATING MID

In his November 7, 1992, scientific presentation to the American College for Advancement in Medicine, Paul Yutsis told his colleagues: "I cannot imagine the treatment of patients suffering from chronic fatigue and immune dysfunction syndrome in the 90s without applying the understanding of metabolic immunodepression to their management!" The following are the six therapeutic stops Dr. Yutsis outlined for reversing MID:

1. Avoid "white" foods, eliminating such poor nutritional items as white sugar, white rice, and white flour from the diet. This not only helps reverse the process of MID, it can help prevent it.

2. Avoid foods that contain yeast and sugar.

3. Stabilize glucose and insulin blood levels nutritionally with the use of orally-administered chromium picolinate and other types of chromium salts, vanadyl sulfate, and selenium.

4. Lower serum cholesterol with nutritional supplementation of Omega-3, Omega-6, and Omega-9 fatty acids, as well as with garlic, other herbal preparations, niacin, and inositol picolinate.

5. Increase vitamins C, B-complex, B_{12}, pantothenic acid, and the minerals chromium, selenium, manganese, zinc, and magnesium intravenously. Add the herbs echinacea root, goldenseal root, St. John's wort, licorice root, astragalus, Siberian ginseng root, and lomatium, all orally administered.

6. Regulate blood insulin levels, lower blood cholesterol, and reduce triglycerides with a series of intravenous infusions of ethylene diamine tetraacetic acid. This treatment, known as chelation therapy, is a powerful antioxidant.

Dr. Yutsis put Laura Maloney through this treatment plan. Although the correction of her pathologies occurred slowly, by the time of her last visit in January 1993, the woman who had suffered from such problems as a yeast infection, hypoglycemia, high levels of triglycerides and LDLs, EBV infection, and a low white blood cell count was no longer feeling or acting disabled. Laboratory examinations showed that 95 percent of her abnormalities were gone.

Today, she lives in a less industrialized part of the country, switched her occupation from bank clerk to seamstress to avoid the effects of high technology, is married and the mother of a healthy girl. Clearly, reversing MID is possible.

PART II

VIRUSES AS COFACTORS OF THE DOWNHILL SYNDROME

Viruses are the smallest and simplest forms of life on earth. Yet human contact with viruses—whose name comes from the Latin for poisonous slime—has led to widespread and sometimes disastrous consequences, such as the 1918 influenza A pandemic that claimed over 30 million lives, and now the international AIDS epidemic, which may claim even more lives.

Since the isolation of the first virus in 1892, scientists have come to further understand these submicroscopic parasites. Most people know that a viral organism is a minute particle too small to be visible with a light microscope and so tiny it can't even be trapped by filters. But they may not know these other facts about viruses.

Each virus consists of a core of nucleic acid—either DNA or RNA—surrounded by a protein shell. But unlike all other life-forms, it contains only one type of this genetic material, never both

DNA and RNA together. The viral organism is not a cell and has no nucleus, no membrane, no cytoplasm; rather, it's merely genetic material cocooned inside the protein coating.

Viruses replicate, but they can only grow inside the cells of other living hosts, including plants, animals, and microorganisms. Without hosts, viruses cannot function as living organisms and cannot cause disease pathology.

The sole function of viruses in life's overall plan becomes one of waiting. They wait to be carried on dust particles, airborne droplets, in the soil, on animal fur, or inside the intestines of insects to invade host animal cells, plant cells, or other microorganisms. When environmental chance allows for such invasion, the viruses leave their nearly lifeless state of suspension and become activated as cellular poisons, promoting disease symptoms.

We now know that viral infection plays an important role in creating or aggravating symptoms of the Downhill Syndrome. The viruses that have been strongly identified with CFIDS include Epstein-Barr virus (EBV); cytomegalovirus (CMV); human herpesvirus type VI (HHV-6); and Retrovirus (mRNA). Their importance in diagnosing and treating the Downhill Syndrome is the focus of Part II.

6.

CHRONIC
EPSTEIN-BARR VIRUS

In the late 1980's, terms such as CFIDS and Downhill Syndrome did not exist. During that time, researchers believed that the disease then known as Chronic Fatigue Syndrome was not only related to the Epstein-Barr Virus (EBV), it was caused by the virus as well. By the 1990's, researchers became fully convinced that the EBV was not the single cause of CFIDS, but is one of the contributing factors of the syndrome. Although EBV is only one of many contributing factors to CFIDS, its role is an important one. Chronic EBV (CEBV) is both complex and misunderstood. Although its primary symptom is chronic fatigue, sufferers will tell you it's a lot more debilitating than that.

A TYPICAL CEBV VICTIM

For months, forty-one-year-old Lydia Wonstad of Seattle, Washington, was in a state of perpetual frustration. Although she suffered from persistent fatigue, no one seemed to believe that she had a real illness. Not even her husband seemed convinced she actually was sick.

Some days, Lydia had all the energy she needed to manage her part-time career as a real estate broker along with her home life, raising four children. Other days, she felt so weak and tired she couldn't rise from bed. At the real estate office, she had trouble remembering people's names, appointments, house prices, contract terms, and other simple things. Throughout the day, she felt pain in her arms and legs, and strange tingling sensations spread up the back of her neck and across her face. In addition, she had recurrent sore throats, headaches, gastrointestinal discomforts, emotional distress, and bouts of depression.

One doctor diagnosed the flu, another said mononucleosis. But months passed, and she just kept feeling worse.

"I visited one doctor after another—chiropractors, naturopaths, homeopaths, body workers—and none of them could find anything wrong after flu and mononucleosis were finally ruled out," Lydia remembers. "Some of them thought it was all in my head. I was devastated by the implied diagnosis that my problems were psychosomatic in origin."

It took six years and the collective expertise of twelve health-care professionals before Lydia Wonstad was able to live again as a nearly healthy person. During that time, her husband divorced her, and their two younger children—unsupervised for so long—got into trouble with the police.

Although chronic fatigue still hounds her, the pain in her arms and legs has disappeared, and her other symptoms have lessened. If she has had any true relief, it's been in knowing that what caused her so much suffering at last has a name. "I know that doesn't sound like a lot," Lydia admits, "but when you've been through so much emotional trauma like me, it's wonderful just to be taken seriously, just to be believed."

THE PHYSIOLOGY OF CEBV

The diagnostic name for Lydia Wonstad's long-term condition is chronic Epstein-Barr virus (CEBV) syndrome. As we've seen, its symptoms include sore throats, generalized inflammation of the lymphatic system, headaches, a vague grippe-like malaise, enlargement of the spleen, and sometimes enlargement of the liver.

EBV is a member of the Herpes group of viruses, which include *Herpes simplex* types I and II, *Varicella zoster virus, Cytomegalovirus,* and *Pseudorabies virus.* A common theme of these viruses is their ability to establish a lifelong latent infection in the human host after the initial infection. This latent infection is usually kept in check by the body's immune system. When the immune system is compromised, however, the infection can become reactivated.

EBV infection is widespread. Between 30 percent and 45 percent

SIGNS AND SYMPTOMS OF CEBV

According to clinical findings, patients diagnosed with CEBV exhibit at least some of the symptoms shown below.

1. Fatigue
   - Intensity varies from completely disabling to more manageable tiredness.
   - Frequency varies from consistent and unchanging to periodic.
2. Pharyngitis (sore throat)—recurrent.
3. Muscle aches (Myalgia)—recurrent.
4. Headaches—recurrent.
5. Depression or unusual mood changes.
6. Insomnia
7. Lack of concentration
8. Anxiety
9. Nausea
10. Swollen lymph glands (lymphadenopathy)
11. Stomachache (gastrointestinal discomfort)
12. Diarrhea
13. Cough
14. Rash
15. Odd skin sensations
16. Loss of appetite
17. Joint Pains (arthralgia)
18. Vomiting
19. Recurrent fevers
20. Intermittent swelling of fingers
21. Unxeplained weight loss or gain
22. History that includes:
    - Mononucleosis
    - Oral herpes
    - Genital herpes
    - Herpes zoster (shingles)
    - Allergies (food, drug, or hay fever)

of adolescents and young adults who are infected with EBV in the United States develop mononucleosis. These are the very people who are fated to come down with symptoms of the Downhill Syndrome.

When the primary infection occurs in childhood, it is usually asymptomatic. When it occurs in adolescence or early adulthood, however, the clinical manifestations of infectious mononucleosis develop in approximately half of the infected people. Transmission or shedding of the virus occurs mainly through saliva and can continue for two to six months after the initial symptoms have subsided. Although the symptoms of infectious mononucleosis usually resolve within several months, the latent infection can periodically reactivate. Therefore, it is almost impossible to prevent transmission of the virus.

DISEASES ASSOCIATED WITH CEBV

Only within the last decade has there been sufficient evidence to implicate EBV in the broad clinical spectrum of CFIDS. Several studies have demonstrated the presence of EBV in patients whose symptoms are those of the Downhill Syndrome.

In the thirty years since the discovery of the EBV in a Ugandan child victimized by Burkitt's lymphoma (a cancer of the lymphatic system), the virus has been associated with an array of disorders, both benign and malignant. Cellular or molecular "snapshots" have allowed scientists to see that diseases such as hairy leukoplakia, mononucleosis, nasopharyngeal carcinoma, Hodgkin's disease, T-cell lymphoma, parotid carcinoma, all of the different Herpes infections, and post-transplantation lymphoma have much in common. The EBV has been found in most patients with these conditions, with chronic fatigue being its most common symptom.

EBV also establishes a lifelong latent infection of a small fraction of B-lymphocytes. In this way, it may be the direct source of the two malignant diseases, Burkitt's lymphoma and nasopharyngeal carcinoma, both rare in the United States but more common in Equatorial Africa.

It is clear that CEBV is a severe condition that warrants specific screening tests and treatments.

SCREENING TESTS AND TREATMENTS FOR CEBV

CEBV is difficult to detect because its symptoms are so maddeningly vague and can apply to such a wide range of disorders. "Many physicians are frustrated by their inability to diagnose it," admits Jack Warren, M.D., head of the Division of Infectious Diseases at the University of Maryland School of Medicine.

Generally, physicians try to rule out other possible causes of distress, such as multiple sclerosis, thyroid disease, and disorders of the immune system. CEBV can be detected, most commonly by blood testing.

DESCRIPTION OF ANTIBODIES DURING
A CEBV INFECTION

In the early stage of CEBV, antibodies of both the immunoglobulin M (IgM) and immunoglobulin G (IgG) classes appear in the patient's blood and peak in three to six days after the onset of infection. These antibodies gradually regress to undetectable levels a few months after symptoms appear, replaced by the anti-nuclear antigen antibodies (anti-EBNAs). After peaking, both the IgG of a different antigen (anti-viral capsid antigen or VCA) and the anti-EBNA generally remain detectable at a low level, and are excellent markers to detect a past a EBV infection.

When anti-VCAs are above the normal range, it is suggestive of a recurrent or reactivated EBV infection, especially when anti-EBNA antibodies are present. In some patients, however, there have been no detectable anti-EBNAs during a suspected reactivation of the infection, making detection even more difficult.

MOST COMMON TESTS FOR CEBV

Since elevated antibody titers could be an important sign of immunological stress and compromise, most physicians order the EBV Panel test. The test readings are sometimes difficult to evaluate because they can be affected by more serious immunological diseases such as Hodgkin's disease, rheumatoid arthritis, and multiple sclerosis.

Physicians usually request that patients undergo a complete

diagnostic laboratory workup and thorough physical examination. These are necessary because the symptoms of CEBV are so similar to those of other diseases. Dr. Gary Holmes of the federal Centers for Disease Control and Prevention suggests:

> *"Physicians caring for patients who are thought to have this [EBV or the Downhill] syndrome should continue to search for more definable and often treatable conditions that may be responsible for their patient's symptoms, including lymphomas and other malignancies; chronic heart, liver, kidney, lung, and endocrine diseases; anxiety and depression; immunodeficiency states; chronic infectious diseases such as tuberculosis; autoimmune diseases; and other chronic inflammatory conditions."*

Once doctors have ruled out other causes for the symptoms, they may carry out the following additional tests for CEBV:

- A *Hemogram.* The hemogram involves an evaluation of the results of the patient's routine blood test, including an estimate of the blood hemoglobin level, the packed cell volume, and the numbers of red and white blood cells. By the second or third week of infection, the total white blood cell count is usually about 15,000 mcL instead of the normal 5,000 to 7,000 mcLs. In addition, a patient with CEBV will show increased numbers of atypical lymphocytes.

- *The Paul-Bunnell-Davidson test.* This blood test detects heterophil antibodies at the third month after chronic fatigue and the other symptoms of the Downhill Syndrome set in.

- *EBV-specific serodiagnostic tests.* These use immunofluorescence techniques to show lymphoblasts (new lymphocytes) from selected cultures that reveal CEBV antigens.

- Tests for *specific IgM antibodies and IgG VCAs* described earlier in this chapter. These procedures lead to the diagnosis of current CEBV in about 95 percent of cases.

- *Liver function tests.* Since liver involvement is not uncommon in CEBV, alkaline phosphatase, SGPT, and SGOT tests should be performed.

MEDICAL CONTROVERSY ABOUT CEBV BLOOD TESTS

In contrast to the information provided here, two studies have reported that persons with CFIDS are no more likely than healthy controls to show EBV antibodies in their blood. Furthermore, although in one study these patients had slightly higher EBV titers (levels of antibody against EBV in the blood) than controls, the two groups overlapped, and the "elevated titers" were of no value in determining the diagnosis or in assessing the status of illness in individual patients. This testing also found similar, slightly higher titers against several other viruses in the patient group, further decreasing the likelihood that EBV was the cause of their illnesses.

The medical controversy continues. It is possible that reactivation of the EBV is a factor in the onset of a symptom complex such as the Downhill Syndrome in some patients but not others. Medical researchers, such as Dr. Paul Cheney continue to pursue this possibility. Other researchers, such as Dr. Gary Holmes, caution that elevated titers of EBV antibodies are frequently found in healthy people and in those with a variety of other diseases. Because of these findings, many medical investigators believe it is unlikely that EBV is the single causal agent of the Downhill Syndrome.

"I believe the EBV will not turn out to be the primary cause of the Downhill Syndrome," says Dr. Anthony Komaroff, Chief of General Medicine at the Brigham & Women's Hospital in Boston, Massachusetts. "It might be that some other virus wakes up the sleeping EBV and one or both may make people sick," he adds.

COMMON TREATMENT FOR CEBV

About the only therapy doctors uniformly prescribe is rest. Some patients have been treated with acyclovir, an anti-viral drug, but there is little proof that this medication eliminates CEBV.

Any strenuous activity must be avoided. Patients are told to take aspirin or other analgesics to control headache and use salt water gargles to relieve sore throats.

Treatment sometimes includes the use of corticosteroids when the CEBV causes airway obstruction, neurologic involvement, hemolytic anemia, thrombocytopenic purpura, myocarditis, or pericarditis. In addition, painkillers and anti-inflammatory drugs have offered some slight symptomatic relief.

WHOLISTIC REMEDIES FOR CEBV

Frustrated with traditional medicines, members of the American College for Advancement in Medicine (ACAM) and the American Academy of Environmental Medicine (AAEM) have turned their attention to more esoteric remedies. Such wholistic physicians suggest that patients minimize stress, get plenty of rest, and improve their nutritional intake by eating fresh foods (especially vegetables, whole grains, and fruits) and taking a variety of nutritional supplements.

Other remedies include acupuncture, bee pollen, modified diets, electrical stimulation, exotic elixirs, megadose vitamins and minerals, herbal extracts, and intravenous (IV) infusions with remedies that build the patient's immune system.

Immune defenses are built up through IV injections with thirty to fifty grams of vitamin C. To activate greater numbers of T-lymphocytes, wholistic doctors employ high doses of vitamins A, B_6, C, and E, the minerals zinc, selenium, and coenzyme Q_{10}.

For activating macrophages, they add to this regimen the non-vitamin bioflavonoid quercitin and an extract synthesized from grapefruit seed pulp, Citricidal, a broad-spectrum antimicrobial compound that is antibacterial, antiparasitic, antifungal, and antiviral.

For increased general protection against viruses, bacteria, and fungi, ACAM and AAEM doctors also recommend adding minerals such as chromium, magnesium, and calcium, and essential oils that include omega-3, omega-6, and omega-9 fatty acids for improving immune system function. Exciting work with other viruses, notably HIV in AIDS, has shown an unexpected value to high-dose phospholipid products, including egg yolk lecithin, in special formulations. All of these items are readily available nonprescription remedies.

7.

THE CYTOMEGALOVIRUS (CMV)

L ike the EBV, CMV is a member of the herpes group of disease organisms. And like that virus, CMV is an important con-tributing factor to the development of CFIDS. It is spread by intimate contact, including kissing, sexual intercourse (in both the semen and cervical secretions), ingesting breast milk, or by contact with infected human blood, secretions, or excretions. Severe disease occurs primarily in an immunosuppressed person, especially in someone with AIDS, cancer, or an individual who has undergone organ transplantation.

THE PREVALENCE OF CMV

CMV affects millions of people around the world. This virus thrives almost anywhere in the human body. The infected person may excrete the virus in urine or saliva for months. Indeed, another medical label for CMV is salivary-gland virus. It ranges in severity from a silent infection without any medical consequences to a dis-ease with such symptoms as overwhelming fatigue, fever, hepatitis, pneumonitis, and (in newborns) severe brain damage, stillbirth, or perinatal death.

The prevalence of CMV increases as the population ages. For individuals, the chances of having a CMV infection increase with the number of sexual partners. In addition, detectable CMV anti-bodies are present in the blood serum of most homosexual men.

High infection rates occur in closed populations such as orphan-ages, schools (especially colleges), hospitals, health clubs, spas, resort communities, and other places where people repeatedly congregate in relatively intimate surroundings. Blood studies indicate that 60 to 90 percent of all adults in Western societies have been infected with CMV, whether with mild or dramatic symptoms.

HOW CMV THRIVES

In her book, *A Dancing Matrix: Voyages Along the Viral Frontier*, Robin Marantz Henig describes the mutation of a latent CMV in an immunosuppressed patient who receives a kidney transplant. The middle-aged patient's new kidney contains CMV that is lying dormant, but her suppressed immune system is unable to impose restrictive control, as would be done in a healthy body. Without continuous surveillance by the immune system's usual marauding cells, called *macrophages*, the CMV reactivates and starts replicating within the patient's new kidney.

"I'm concerned that the chances for mutation increase with the number of generations," says Edwin D. Kilbourne, M.D., a virologist at the Mt. Sinai School of Medicine in New York City. The patient's immunosuppression, he says, "provides increased replication possibilities. If the virus has a chance more and more to flourish in the tissues of the adult, then it's possible that new tropisms can emerge, and new virulence, and new transmission patterns." Henig concludes that CMV may then turn into a highly dangerous infectant.

THE CMV/CFIDS CONNECTION

People suffering from the Downhill Syndrome hardly ever suspect CMV as a source of the symptom of devastating fatigue. Yet it is important to recognize the possibility of CMV as a primary source of common Downhill Syndrome symptoms. If the immune system becomes suppressed, as we've seen in many CFIDS patients, CMV can become extremely active, creating further suppression of the immune system and intensified CFIDS symptoms.

An acute illness with fever, usually referred to as CMV mononucleosis or CMV hepatitis, may result from a CMV infection. The patient's fever often lasts for two to three weeks, and jaundice and a rash may develop. Acute fatigue turns to chronic fatigue, the main diagnostic sign of the condition.

Frequently, CMV infection makes the body vulnerable to other contributing factors of CFIDS such as EBV. When several contributing factors invade the body at once, they work together to further suppress the immune system, triggering the continuous and debilitating cycle of CFIDS symptoms.

THE THREE CLASSICAL SYNDROMES OF CMV

The symptoms and signs of acute CMV infection frequently show up in the form of three medically recognized syndromes. These syndromes are important for all CFIDS patients to understand because acute CMV disease can, either immediately or later on in life, turn into chronic CMV infection, contributing to the symptoms of the Downhill Syndrome.

1. *Cytomegalovirus inclusion disease* and perinatal disease. These are two components of intrauterine infection of infants whose mothers have experienced a primary infection with CMV during pregnancy. The neonatal symptoms include jaundice, liver enlargement, and abnormally small numbers of platelets in the circulating blood, among others. Diagnosis may be confirmed by finding viruses in the urine within the first week after birth, or by detecting IgM antibodies to CMV in the blood.

2. *Acute acquired Cytomegalovirus infection.* This is a syndrome similar to EBV-associated infectious mononucleosis. It is characterized by fever, malaise, muscle pains, and joint pains. With this syndrome, atypical lymphocytes are found in the blood, and liver function is affected.

Transmission can be by sexual contact, respiratory droplets among nursery or day-care-center attendants, and transfusions of blood, which is why we caution readers to avoid blood transfusions if possible. Transmission of acute CMV also occurs from drinking milk taken from cow udders injected with recombinant bovine growth hormone (rBGH) to produce more milk.

3. *Disease in immunocompromised hosts.* People who have had tissue or bone transplants run great risk from CMV infection. Increased risk for viral infection is especially dominant during the first 100 days after transplantation. HIV-infected patients may show a variety of CMV manifestations, since CMV is itself immunosup-

pressive and may worsen symptoms of HIV infection itself.

DIAGNOSING CMV INFECTION

The best way to diagnose a CMV infection is to isolate the virus, as well as to take urine cultures and blood tests like the indirect fluorescent antibody and the anticomplement immunofluorescent antibody.

CMV cannot be grown in laboratory animals or in most nonhuman cell cultures for laboratory examination. The result is that no specific diagnostic laboratory test or therapy exists for this chronic fatigue problem.

The appearance of certain antibodies during acute illness provides some supportive evidence of its presence. Most of the time, however, a clinical diagnosis is made by the physician from medical history and a physical examination. CMV's major symptoms are physical and mental exhaustion and enlargement of the liver.

Since confusion with EBV is not uncommon, physicians test for pharyngitis (inflammation of the pharynx), lymphadenopathy (swelling and tenderness of the lymph nodes), and positive EBV heterophil antibodies. Absence of all three indicates primary CMV mononucleosis rather than EBV. Additionally, the presence of CMV antibodies confirms a diagnosis of CMV infection.

TREATMENT FOR CMV INFECTION

At present, traditional physicians have little to treat the CMV infection. If doctors detect retinitis, they frequently prescribe the generic drug ganciclovir, the first antiviral agent licensed in the United States for use against life- or sight-threatening infections caused by CMV. This drug has improved symptoms of CMV retinitis in patients with AIDS.

Other standard generic drugs such as floxuridine and cytarabine may be used to stop viral DNA synthesis. But both of these drugs are highly toxic, and must be administered with great caution.

There are several alternative treatments used by wholistic physicians who belong to the American College for the Advancement in Medicine and the American Academy of Environmental Medicine. These treatments attempt to strengthen the patient's ability to fight off the disease using his or her own immune system. These physicians have had success with some little-known techniques such as ozone therapy, intravenous infusion of hydrogen peroxide, herbal remedies, traditional Chinese medical techniques, chelation therapy, and megadoses of various nutrients. These therapeutic techniques will be discussed in detail in later chapters.

8.

THE HUMAN HERPESVIRUS-VI (HHV-6)

Herpesviruses, among the most persistent and resistant of infectious organisms, are the source of more illness than any other human viruses. Although the herpesvirus may be best known as the cause of a worldwide epidemic of venereal disease, this family of microorganisms plagues people of all ages and circumstances: the fetus may be devastated by CMV, the child bespotted by chicken pox, the adolescent felled by infectious mononucleosis, the adult pestered by recurrent cold sores, the aged agonized by shingles, and sexually active adults severely limited in their intimate pleasures by uncontrolled genital herpes.

Now, another recently discovered herpes organism is producing serious pathology for the populace: the Human Herpesvirus-VI (HHV-6). And, as we will see, it is implicated as a contributor to the Downhill Syndrome.

DISCOVERING HHV-6

In 1986, top microbiological researcher S. Zaki Salahuddin, Ph.D., and other scientists associated with Robert C. Gallo, M.D., in the Tumor Cell Biology lab at the National Cancer Institute in Bethesda, Maryland, discovered a previously unknown herpesvirus. HHV-6 became the first new herpesvirus to be identified since Dr. M. Anthony Epstein and Dr. Yvonne M. Barr reported on the existence of the Epstein-Barr virus in 1964.

It took almost twenty-two years from one viral discovery to the next, but revealing the existence of HHV-6 was directly linked to ongoing research on AIDS. The virulent human immunodeficiency virus (HIV), first isolated in AIDS patients with depressed immune systems, provided an extraordinary human research laboratory for unearthing other viruses.

THE HHV-6/CFIDS CONNECTION

Researchers are now focusing on how HHV-6 may be a prime contributor to the symptoms associated with the Downhill Syndrome, especially chronic fatigue. What they've found is that this newest of the various herpes organisms targets the immune system's B lymphocytes (B cells) and its T lymphocytes (T cells). CFIDS researchers such as Anthony L. Komaroff, M.D., of Brigham and Women's Hospital in Boston, Massachusetts, speculate that this HHV-6 organism upsets the delicate balance between the EBV and the immune system, awakening EBV from its latent state. Also, the HHV-6 is implicated in the activation of the CMV latent in most Americans.

In a meeting hosted by the Centers for Disease Control in September 1991, researchers designated three viruses as the most likely causes of the Downhill Syndrome: HHV-6, and two cancer-causing retroviruses, HTLV-II (human T-cell lymphotropic virus) and the human foamy virus.

During laboratory testing of some 300 Downhill Syndrome patients from Incline Village, Boston, Bethesda, and elsewhere, National Institutes of Health researchers found that HHV-6 antibodies were present in the patients' blood, indicating that these people possessed either a latent or active infection more than 80 percent of the time.

A majority of nearly all the populations living in Western industrialized nations possesses antibodies to HHV-6, meaning that most people in these countries have sustained infections from it. Since the organism can be isolated from saliva, this virus probably is transmitted by coughing, kissing, and other forms of contact with upper respiratory tract secretions. Up to 92 percent of healthy adults shed the virus in their saliva, so that when somebody sneezes on you, it's more than likely that HHV-6 has been transferred to your respiratory system. Fortunately for the majority of these adults, infection will only develop in people with immunosuppression.

POSSIBLE LINKS BETWEEN
CLINICAL DISEASES AND HHV-6

A growing number of disorders are now recognized as caused or triggered by HHV-6 invasion, and these are tied indirectly to symptoms associated with the Downhill Syndrome. These disorders represent an acute HHV-6 infection. Once a person has recovered, the virus becomes dormant, waiting for an opportunity to thrive again. This can occur when the immune system becomes suppressed. Even a disorder in childhood caused by HHV-6 can be a contributor to the development many years later of CFIDS.

The disorders include:

- *Roseola,* an illness of infants and young children, which manifests itself with an abrupt, high fever, sore throat, and swollen lymph nodes. Seizures during its onset may occur. After four or five days the fever drops to normal and a faint, pink, pimple-like rash appears on the child's neck, body, and thighs. The rash may last a few hours to two days.

Many virologists and other researchers conducting studies, including those undertaken in Japan, England, and Finland, have reported that HHV-6 has been isolated from the patients' blood while they were in the acute stage of roseola and during convalescence from it. Therefore, it has been tempting to link HHV-6 infection with roseola. Research on this link continues.

- *Other childhood fever and rash illnesses* have had HHV-6 identified in the patients' blood, especially when the victims were between ages three months and three years.

- *Hepatitis A and B,* two forms of liver inflammation involving yellowing of the skin, enlarged liver, loss of appetite, stomach discomfort, and abnormal liver function, may be triggered by an acute HHV-6 infection.

- *Infectious mononucleosis-like illnesses* (which have symptoms similar to infectious mononucleosis). Blood tests on patients with mononucleosis show elevated antibodies of HHV-6. These raised levels appear even in patients with acute EBV- or CMV-related mononucleosis. According to investigators, the elevated antibody count levels may have come on as a result of reactivation of previously latent HHV-6 infections.

• *Chronic fatigue patients* invariably show a higher prevalence of HHV-6 antibodies in the blood, but as yet there has been no conclusive link between the virus and chronic fatigue.

Much needs to be learned about this relatively new organism and its role in diseases. Although it is not proven as a complicating infectious factor in the Downhill Syndrome, ridding the body of HHV-6 would help solve the patient's difficulties with chronic fatigue and its associated symptoms.

A STRONG DISEASE LINK

In the August 15, 1992 *Annals of Internal Medicine,* three viral disease researchers drew a parallel between CFIDS in patients infected with HHV-6 and Sjogren syndrome (or Sjogren disease). They suggested that an overlapping series of symptoms may exist or that some CFIDS patients may actually possess the Sjogren syndrome alone; consequently, treatment of this disorder may be useful in conquering CFIDS, too.

Sjogren syndrome is a chronic, systemic inflammatory disorder of unknown cause, most often seen in menopausal women. It is characterized by dryness of the mouth, eyes, and other mucous membranes; patients suffer with such rheumatic disorders as rheumatoid arthritis, scleroderma, and systemic lupus erythematosis.

Connecting the two syndromes, doctors from the Johns Hopkins Medical Institutions and the Francis Scott Key Hospital in Baltimore, Maryland, write: "The potential relation between the Sjogren syndrome with central nervous system disease and neurologic disease in the chronic fatigue syndrome needs further investigation. Because the former is an immunologic disorder that is responsive to immunosuppressive therapy, this diagnostic distinction has important therapeutic implications."

TREATMENT OF HHV-6

Although clinical trials have not yet been performed with certain antiviral drugs, there is a suspicion among virologists that HHV-6 infection probably does react positively to such antiviral drugs as ganciclovir, phosphonoformate, and foscarnet.

In a 1991 study involving a group of ninety-two Downhill Syndrome patients, half of the group received Ampligen, an experimental antivirus drug, for six months, while the control group was given a placebo. Those taking the Ampligen recovered almost fully; those who received the placebo did not improve at all.

HHV-6, along with other herpesviruses such as EBV and CMV, has found a way to infect us and remain with us for a lifetime, invading our immune defenses and evolving complex mechanisms for reactivation when these defenses become suppressed. Such a destruction of our normal immune functioning sets the stage for the symptoms of CFIDS.

9.

HUMAN RETROVIRUSES AS DISEASE FACTORS

If by now you have the impression that people are succumbing to numerous viral diseases caused by some new pathological organisms, you are correct. In fact, there is a recently discovered category of viruses designated by virologists most familiar with them as "submicroscopic hijackers," "pirates of the cell," or "pieces of bad news wrapped up in protein." Such organisms have been categorized in the viral family known as the *retroviridae* or *retroviruses*. People who have these retroviruses experience debilitating fatigue and flu-like afflictions. Although some researchers discount the connection between retroviruses and CFIDS, other researchers believe there is a strong possibility that retroviruses are an important factor in the disease.

The search for retroviruses heated up in the fall of 1990, as a result of discoveries made by Elaine DeFreitas, Ph.D., the virologist from the Wistar Institute in Philadelphia introduced in Chapter One. Dr. DeFreitas had linked CFIDS to free-floating pieces of RNA that transform into DNA. Using their own special enzymes, the reverse transcriptases, these retroviruses are able to splice themselves permanently into the chromosomes of human host cells and turn back upon the cells (that's what makes them "retro" or "reversing").

Remember that each virus consists of a core of nucleic acid—either DNA or RNA—surrounded by a protein shell, and that unlike all other life forms, it contains only one type of this genetic material, never both DNA and RNA together. Most viruses store their genetic information in DNA.

THE DIFFERENCE BETWEEN
VIRUSES AND RETROVIRUSES

How do retroviruses differ from other types of viral organisms?

While all other viruses store their genetic information in DNA and copy it into RNA (the mRNA, to be specific), the retroviruses do the opposite. Retroviruses have their genetic information on RNA and copy it into DNA using the enzyme *reverse transcriptase* (RT). The DNA is then transcribed into RNA.

Thus, starting with a single plus-strand RNA gene strand, retroviruses copy this RNA strand into another double strand of DNA. That DNA, in turn, is transcribed and synthesized into the messenger RNA, or mRNA, that becomes packaged into the virus offspring. The "beauty" of the retroviruses is that they constantly give off new genetic information, making it difficult for the immune system to recognize them.

The family of retroviruses are grouped in three subfamilies: Oncovirinae (the RNA tumor viruses), Spumavirinae (the foamy viruses), and Lentivirinae (the "slow" viruses of sheep and human T-cell lymphotropic viruses or HTLV). Scientists studying the connection between retroviruses and CFIDS have mostly concentrated on the foamy viruses and HTLV.

THE FOAMY RETROVIRUS

Researchers have long been intrigued, and a bit unnerved, by the retroviral subfamily of microbes known as spuma or "foamy" viruses. Spuma viruses are described as foamy because they induce extensive fluid-filled spaces within the host cells that they infect.

W. John Martin, M.D., Ph.D., chief of molecular immunopathology at the University of Southern California Medical Center, Los Angeles, has linked the mysterious foamy retrovirus to several of the symptoms of the Downhill Syndrome, including severe fatigue, insomnia, and joint and muscle pains. Dr. Martin found foamy retroviruses in 160 out of 300 patients diagnosed with CFIDS. In addition, his finding of this same virus in a recent spate of severe, unexplained neurological illnesses is significant because many people afflicted with the Downhill Syndrome suffer some kind of unexplained neurological problems.

Four separate research teams have confirmed Dr. Martin's findings by detecting the foamy viral infection among patients with CFIDS. In separate investigations, both Dr. Martin and Dr. DeFreitas have succeeded in extracting whole human foamy viruses from patients showing symptoms of the Downhill Syndrome. But there is still a long way to go before researchers will make a definitive connection between retroviruses and CFIDS.

"More research must follow to determine if the foamy retrovirus is indeed infectious, and if it causes chronic fatigue syndrome. This is just the beginning," says Dr. DeFreitas.

Dr. Martin has been studying CFIDS since 1988, when local specialists started sending him patients with strange brain conditions. The first patient he studied was a teacher who, after deteriorating for nine months, was unable to write, draw, or perform arithmetic. In fact, she couldn't even draw a picture of a clock face containing numbers. When he applied genetic probes to a sample of her brain tissue, Dr. Martin discerned an "atypical viral infection." The examined tissue tested negatively for such likely suspects as herpesviruses, but it responded positively to a general probe for retroviruses. Dr. Martin got similar results when he tested blood and spinal fluid from several other neurology patients.

Scientists at the CDC are also verifying the retroviral connection. One such scientist, virologist Walter Gunn, M.D., admits that linking the Downhill Syndrome to an unusual virus won't allay the epidemic. No one knows whether the infection will turn out to be a cause or a cofactor in the illness. And even if a causal role is confirmed, the task will remain to figure out how the virus spreads and how to stop it.

ON THE TRAIL OF OTHER RETROVIRUSES

Many of the infectious viruses discussed reside in most people, but they are held in check by their immune systems. Jay A. Levy, Ph.D., a biomedical researcher working at the University of California in San Francisco, has shown that victims of the Downhill Syndrome possess abnormal immune systems that fail to clear the body of invading viruses, or to prevent reactivation of latent ones. Together with Nancy Klimas, Ph.D., an immunologist at the University of Miami School of Medicine, Dr. Levy has raised the question of whether Downhill Syndrome patients with failing immune systems are showing the cause or effect of their affliction.

Drs. Klimas and Levy compared 147 people affected by the Downhill Syndrome with 145 healthy people in a control group. They reported that patients with severe chronic fatigue symptoms have abnormalities in a group of infection-fighting lymphocytes known as CD_8 cells. Although the CFIDS patients showed increased numbers of CD_8 killer cells that launch an attack on an invader, they also showed lower-than-normal amounts of CD_8 suppressor cells that are supposed to damp the immune system after the system's job is done. The result is not good. The patients end up with a hyperactive immune system that pours uncontrolled amounts of agents called cytokines into the body, provoking fatigue, muscle pain, and other flu-like symptoms.

After performing blood tests on both groups, Dr. Levy found no correlation between any of several viruses and chronic fatigue. One question the researchers are investigating is whether an unidentified retrovirus is involved in killing the suppressor cells that would moderate the action of the immune system.

Ten scientists, participating in research sponsored by the Wistar Institute in Philadelphia, have been investigating at least two human T cell retroviruses, HTLV-1 and HTLV-2, as possible causative agents of the Downhill Syndrome.

The scientists compared thirty adults and children with severe symptoms of the Downhill Syndrome to twenty healthy people. The investigators, led by Dr. Elaine DeFreitas, Dr. Paul R. Cheney, and Dr. David S. Bell, found that more than 50 percent of the blood samples from sick patients contained antibodies to at least two viral gene products, while the blood samples from the healthy control group contained no such antibodies. "The frequency of those antibodies in CFIDS patients compared with healthy, noncontact controls suggests exposure/infection with an HTLV-like agent rare in healthy noncontact people," wrote the investigators.

While HTLV-reactive antibodies were present in the Downhill Syndrome patients, the investigators would not definitely blame retroviruses as the source of their disease. The investigators concluded:

"Although our data support an association between an HTLV-like agent and CFIDS, we cannot, as yet, define the agent's role in the disease process. Rather than an etiologic [causative] agent, it may be a benign secondary infection to which immunologically compromised patients are susceptible. Alternatively, it may be one of two viruses that, when coinfecting the same hematopoetic [blood] cells, induce immune dysfunction. In any case, biological characterization of this agent and its role in the pathogenesis of CFIDS awaits its isolation."

THE CDC FINDINGS ON THE
RETROVIRUS/CFIDS CONNECTION

As a result of the research by Drs. DeFreitas, Cheney, Bell, and their group, the CDC investigated twenty-one Georgia patients for known human retroviruses as the source of their diagnosed CFIDS.

The investigators reported that their blood examinations "yielded no evidence supporting infection with any of the examined retroviruses as a primary cause of or a cofactor in chronic fatigue syndrome [CFS]. . . . Health care providers should not suggest to patients with CFS that convincing evidence exists for an association of their illness with retroviral infection."

Medical investigators spent more than a decade trying to unravel the mysteries of CFIDS by looking into different viruses as a possible cause. In 1990, they thought they had found what they were looking for when Dr. DeFreitas pointed out the CFIDS/retrovirus connection. Although research continues, results point to retroviruses as cofactors in the disease, ones that work hard to make sure the symptoms of the Downhill Syndrome will develop.

10.

POTENTIAL CURES FOR VIRAL INFECTIONS

B oth conventional and wholistic researchers have been searching for ways to eliminate viruses, or at least offer relief from their symptoms. Although there are drugs available from conventional physicians, they often do as much harm as good. The same antiviral drug that inhibits viral growth also suppresses the immune system. Wholistic physicians, who opt for natural treatments, however, are finding more success with a variety of natural remedies.

THE POSSIBILITIES FOR INTERFERON

There is one group of natural products with antimicrobial activity that is accepted enthusiastically by both the conventional and wholistic worlds of medicine: *interferon (IFN)*. IFN, comprised of glycoproteins (antiviral proteins) produced by several different types of mammalian cells infected with one or more viruses, has the ability to inhibit viral growth.

First discovered by Drs. A. Isaacs and J. Lindenmann in 1957, IFNs were touted during the late 1980s as potential magic bullets against cancer. In this past decade, researchers have found that IFN's ability is not so unlimited.

IFN is active against many different viruses. In fact, these proteins are the body's own antivirals, secreted by infected cells to protect healthy cells in their vicinity. Particular interferons work only in the same animal species that produces them. Therefore, it is impossible to build up medicinal quantities of interferons in animals to store for human use.

There are three known interferons: IFN alpha and IFN beta of Type I and IFN gamma (immune interferon) of Type II. IFN alpha is produced by leukocytes (white blood cells) and IFN beta is synthesized by nonleukocytic cells, including fibroblasts. IFN gamma is produced during immune reactions such as those caused by exposure to antigens, mitogens, large granular lymphocytes, or by the lectin-stimulated T-lymphocytes.

Interferons work as antiviral agents even in immunodeficient people, but their effects have not always been shown to be beneficial. In tests on mice, an overzealous antiviral response to IFN alpha or IFN beta has been shown to trigger antibodies against the body's own cells and tissues.

Physicians are using IFN to treat a variety of viruses, and CFIDS-associated viruses have shown some positive response to a treatment of oral administration, intramuscular, and intravenous injections of IFN. However, overall statistics show a 33 percent success rate from interferon treatment.

WHOLISTIC REMEDIES

In contrast to the limited number of virus-inhibiting drugs available through conventional medicine, wholistic practitioners offer a vast array of antiviral remedies derived from natural sources, available without prescription to consumers in health-food stores and some pharmacies. These remedies, which improve the body's ability to fight viral infections, are used successfully by many physicians.

One such physician is Laurence Badgley, M.D., of San Bruno, California. Discussing nutrition as the fundamental instrument in an ill person's immune-boosting armaments, Dr. Badgley writes: "Without a good nutritional program, all other natural therapy applications are doomed to failure. The relationship of nutrition to the immune system is unquestioned...."

Recommended Diet

Dr. Badgley and other physicians, including the authors, recommend following a diet with only unprocessed foods. This diet recommends that followers:

- Eliminate any foods that can cause allergic reactions, or rotate foods so that foods someone is allergic to are only consumed at certain times.

- Eliminate all simple sugars, such as those contained in candy and other sweet foods.

- Avoid high-fat foods, such as ice cream and red meat.

- Avoid all other refined food products.

- Emphasize whole, natural foods that inhibit the growth of viruses, including raw fruits, unflavored yogurt, garlic, onions, scallions, and cruciferous vegetables such as broccoli, cabbage, cauliflower, and brussels sprouts.

In addition, wholistic doctors recommend both vitamin and mineral supplements.

Supplemental Vitamins

The following vitamins, taken in capsules, tablets, liquids, or other forms, should be used daily:

Vitamin C (ascorbic acid), a powerful T-lymphocyte cell stimulator and catalyst of interferon production, should be taken daily in dosages of 3,000 mg or more; higher doses, even those approaching 10,000 mg, may be used provided the person's bowels can tolerate the higher dosage.

Vitamin A, a strong free-radical scavenger, promotes germ-killing enzymes in a divided starting dose of 50,000 IU per day. The standard maintenance dose may level off to 25,000 IU daily.

Vitamin E (d-alpha tocopherol) quenches free radicals and enhances immune response to viruses in a dose of about 1,200 IU per day. (The correct vitamin E dose is measured at 400 IUs for every 40 pounds of body weight.)

Vitamin B complex, agents for vital chemical reactions in the body, is essential for increased energy.

Supplemental Minerals

Minerals are a mandatory part of any viral-control process. Supplementation involves taking twelve particular nutrients at the very least, including zinc, magnesium, potassium, selenium, chromium, calcium, and half-a-dozen others, as determined by hair mineral analysis.

Supplemental Amino Acids

Of the twenty-two amino acids needed to build our numerous protein body structures, nine are essential and may only be acquired from protein. Amino acids aid in the production of antibodies, support the immune system, and stimulate T-lymphocyte activity.

Other Substances

ABAVCA: This natural plant extract improves the ratio between the CD_4 helper cell and the CD_8 suppressor cell lymphocyte. This balance, in turn, helps correct anemia, improve appetite, and reverse swollen glands in patients with viral diseases.

Carnivora®: Extracted from the Venus Fly Trap plant, this medicinal liquid has potent antiviral properties. In fact, Helmut Keller, M.D., of Bad Steben, Germany, the discoverer of the extracted Carnivora antiviral benefits, reports excellent therapeutic results among his patients who are HIV- positive.

Coenzyme Q_{10}: Also known as *ubiquinone*, this vitamin-like substance plays a crucial role in supporting and strengthening the immune system. It should be taken regularly by anyone sitting before a video-display terminal, or who is in touch with other forms of immune system-suppressing non-ionizing radiation for lengthy periods of time. The average dose is 150 mg to 180 mg a day, divided into three doses.

Monolaurin: This component of the fatty acid *laurate* stimulates wide-spectrum antifungal and antiviral activity. The average dose of monolaurin is one or two capsules, taken two to three times daily.

Cat's Claw: Research on the benefits of this herb, found in the Peruvian rain forest, has been conducted at the University of Munich, the Huntington Research Center in England, the Central Research Institute of Chemistry in Hungary, and at the Universities of Naples and Milan. Cat's Claw is one of the most promising herbal remedies for immune dysfunction, and is a potent antiviral substance.

Botanical Medicines: Remedies from the plant kingdom have been known as healing agents for centuries but only now are being recognized for their superior therapeutic qualities. Common ones used in overcoming viral infections are dandelion, golden seal root, ginkgo biloba, silymarin, and burdock root. Of them all, *echinacea* is probably most effective against viral organisms connected with the Downhill Syndrome.

Ingesting *Echinacea arabinogalactan* or *Echinacea angustifolia* has been found to stimulate phagocytes (a special type of immune cell) to gobble up different microbes, including viruses. The herb enhances immunity. In the case of viral infections, increased immunity could speed the clearance of mutant viral strains that might otherwise escape immune detection until they had multiplied to significant numbers.

Echinacea may be obtained in the form of plant root, tincture, fluid extract, or solid extract. Naturopathic physician Patrick M. Donovan offers these viral treatment dosages and their forms for *Echinacea angustifolia:* When using dried root, take 1 to 2 grams (g) three times per day; when using a tincture in an alcohol solution of 1 to 10, take 8 to 12 milliliters (ml) three times per day; when using the fluid extract, take 1.5 to 3.0 ml three times per day; when using a solid extract in a ratio of 6.5 to 1, take 250 milligrams (mg) three times per day.

These other antiviral herbal remedies may reduce or eliminate the symptoms of viral infection:

Hydrastis canadensis
- Dried root: 0.5 to 1.0 g three times per day
- Tincture (1:10): 6 to 12 ml three times per day
- Fluid extract (1:1): 1 to 2 ml three times per day
- Solid extract (4:1): 250 mg three times per day

Phytolacca decandra-americana
- Dried root: 100 to 600 mg three times per day
- Tincture (1:10): 0.2 to 0.6 ml three times per day

Baptisia tinctoria
- Dried root: 0.5 to 1.0 g three times per day
- Tincture (1:5): 2 to 5 ml three times per day
- Fluid extract (1:1): 1 to 2 ml three times per day
- Solid extract (4:1): 250 mg three times per day

The liberal consumption of certain teas made from botanicals has proven beneficial for relieving viral disease symptoms. Try drinking tea made from boneset *(Eupatorium perfoliatum)*, German chamomile *(Matricaria chamomilla)*, burdock *(Arctium lappa)*, or yarrow *(Achillea millefolium)*.

These antiviral herbal remedies have been found to have about a 20 percent success rate in reducing viral symptoms.

Intravenous Infusions

As standard treatment, wholistic practioners include IV infusions with such nutrients as vitamins C, B_1, B_6, B_{12}, pantothenic acid, minerals, and other liquid immune-enhancing substances. These infusions have been demonstrated to reduce the symptoms of the Downhill Syndrome.

The communities of conventional physicians and their wholistic counterparts recently arrived at a rare mutual agreement that declared: "Systemic administration of toxic and ineffective substances such as the generic drug Cytosine Arabinoside and Idoxuridine for the treatment of herpes infections is unwarranted and possibly criminal." This statement pertains to all viruses as well.

Natural remedies, however, have been shown to be effective. Hundreds of wholistic physicians have given anecdotal reports that, unlike synthetic antiviral drugs that suppress the immune system, natural antiviral remedies stimulate the defense system to fight invasion.

PART III

OTHER COFACTORS OF THE DOWNHILL SYNDROME

As we have already seen, the Downhill Syndrome is a condition that is multifactored. That is, there is a wide variety of factors that can induce symptoms or aggravate ones that are already plaguing a person. In addition to the viral factors, there are the factors of yeast, pollutants, dental amalgams, parasites, allergies, hypothyroidism, and others. These are the focus of Part III of The Downhill Syndrome.

11.

THE FACTOR OF
YEAST IN CFIDS

Yeast is a fungus that lives naturally in our bodies. It is normally controlled by the body's immune defenses and by the usual bacterial flora present in the body. When a change affects the homeostasis of the body, helpful bacteria tend to decrease and immune response becomes depressed. That's when a particular type of yeast known as *Candida albicans* and other candida species begin to thrive, especially in the colon. When they invade various parts of the body, the resulting infection is called *candidiasis*. As we will see, candidiasis plays an important role as a cofactor in the symptoms of CFIDS.

THE POTENTIAL DAMAGE OF CANDIDIASIS

Sixty years ago, doctors identified *Candida albicans* as a frequent cause of infections in the vagina, mouth, throat, and gastrointestinal tract. Now, the fungus is known to affect almost all body parts, organs, tissues, and cells. Invading yeast colonies do their damage by releasing powerful chemicals called *canditoxins*, which may be absorbed into the bloodstream, causing such widely diverse symptoms as severe menstrual cramps, lethargy, chronic diarrhea, bladder irritations and infections, asthma, migraines, depression, skin eruptions such as athlete's foot and psoriasis, chronic generalized fatigue, muscle weakness, poor memory, lost sex drive, and persistent coughs.

Research physicians believe that yeast may be a complicating factor in conditions such as AIDS, a contributor to early death in various forms of cancer (especially leukemia), a source of infertility, and a component of multiple sclerosis, myasthenia gravis, disseminated lupus erythematosis, schizophrenia, arthritis, and many other degenerative diseases.

WHY YEAST BECOMES A PROMOTER OF DISEASE

Candida albicans, like the other eighty yeast strains, has about thirty-five antigens, potentially dangerous foreign substances against which the body produces antibodies. When too much yeast has invaded, the antigens outnumber the antibodies, making it difficult for the body to ward off disease.

High technology can cause this explosion of yeast in the body, as can a diet high in animal protein, which is injected with antibiotics. Drugs such as broad-spectrum antibiotics, cortisone, birth control pills, or other steriod derivatives are food for the yeast organism, helping it to reproduce and steadily increase its total area of tissue invasion.

Therapeutic hormones such as estrogen, anti-inflammatory drugs, recreational drugs, foods high in mold or yeast such as cake, bread, beer, mushrooms, and brewer's yeast, plus excess refined sugar or simple carbohydrates—all these promote yeast production. Of these, simple carbohydrates or sugars are the main food on which Candida albicans thrives.

DIAGNOSING CANDIDIASIS

How do you know that you are infected with Candida albicans? Testing for allergies to fungus, yeast, and mold can uncover unsuspected invasion, since allergies and candidiasis are often allied.

Traditional skin pricks, patch tests, scratch tests, and blood tests employed by establishment-type allergists belonging to the American Academy of Allergy and Immunology usually fail to reveal the presence of candidiasis. Since these allergists' conventional methods of testing fail to show the yeast infection, they are likely to declare that there is no such condition.

Rather than using clinical examinations or laboratory tests, wholistic physicians usually make a diagnosis of candidiasis on the basis of a patient's history and symptoms. The following survey, given by a doctor oriented to candidiasis, is probably the best diagnositic tool.

Survey for Candidiasis

There are four questionnaires, one for adults and teenagers in general, another for women only, a third for men only, and a fourth for children under ten. More than three positive responses for either of the first three questionnaires may indicate that candidiasis is a causative factor of the symptoms and signs of the Downhill Syndrome. For the fourth questionnaire, any positive response is an indication that a child could have candidiasis. Candidiasis and CFIDS are not uncommon among children and adolescents. Candidiasis can also be found in children with chronic ear infections, hyperactivity, and asthma. Naturally, the higher the score for any of the questionnaires, the more certain it is that discomforts are caused by *Candida albicans*.

A. Questions for Adults and Teenagers

Have you suffered from:

1. Frequent infections or constant skin problems?

2. Feelings of fatigue, being drained, or drowsiness?

3. Feelings of anxiety, irritability, or insomnia?

4. Strong cravings for sugary foods, breads, or alcoholic beverages?

5. Illness symptoms on damp muggy days, or in moldy places such as a basement?

6. Food sensitivities or allergy reactions?

7. Digestive problems, bloating, heartburn, constipation, or bad breath?

8. Feeling "spacey" or "unreal," difficulty concentrating, or bothered by perfumes, chemical fumes, tobacco smoke?

9. Poor coordination, muscle weakness, or joints painful or swollen?

10. Mood swings, depression, or loss of sexual feelings?

11. Dry mouth or throat, nose congestion or drainage, feeling of pressure above the ears, or frequent headaches?

12. Pains in the chest, shortness of breath, dizziness, or easy bruising?

13. Have you taken antibiotics, birth-control pills, or cortisone medications frequently or over a long duration?

B. Questions for Women Only

Have you suffered from:

1. Vaginal burning or itching, discharge, infections, or urinary problems?

2. Difficulty getting pregnant?

3. Been pregnant two or more times?

4. Taken birth control pills?

5. Premenstrual symptoms such as moodiness, fluid retention, tension?

6. Irregular menstrual cycles or other menstrual problems?

7. Changes in the time or frequency of menstruation (in women of child-bearing age)?

8. Heavy discharge from your nipples?

9. Pain during sexual intercourse?

10. Vaginal spotting?

11. Pelvic pain?

12. Breast lumps?

13. Symptoms of menopause (hot flashes, vaginal dryness, unusual sweating, or insomnia)?

C. Questions for Men Only

Have you suffered from:

1. Difficulty having an erection?

2. A lump in the testicles?

3. A sore on the penis?

4. Any discharge from the penis?

5. A breast lump?

6. Impotence or premature ejaculation?

7. Peyronie's disease (hardening of the penis that causes distortion)?

8. Loss of libido?

9. Prostatitis (inflammation of the prostate)?

10. Testiculitis (inflammation of the testicles)?

11. Pain in the lower abdomen?

D. Questions for Children Under Ten

Has the child suffered from:

1. Frequent infections, particularly tonsilitis, bronchitis, ear infections, or chronic diaper rash?

2. Continuous nasal congestion or drainage?

3. Dark circles under the eyes, periods of hyperactivity, or poor attention span?

4. A long history of bedwetting?

5. Eczema?

Once the problem has been diagnosed, the next step is, of course, treatment.

TREATMENTS FOR CANDIDIASIS

Wholistic doctors are using a variety of successful techniques to treat yeast overgrowth, based on each patient's history and response to therapy. What follows are some natural, safe, and non-toxic candidiasis treatments:

- Avoidance of prescribed therapeutic antibiotics, unless their need to overcome a bacterial infection becomes absolutely mandatory.

- Discontinuance of birth control pills, especially if a vaginal discharge is present or if headaches accompany menstrual periods.

- Application of homeopathic dilutions of candida.

- Consumption of aged garlic extract acquired from a health food store, or the eating of one to two fresh garlic cloves a day.

- Introduction of allergy injections that include antigens contain-

ing Tricophyton-Candida-Epidermophyton (TCE) combined
with different molds to stimulate immune defense responses and
decrease sensitivity to the molds.

- Avoidance of drugs that suppress the immune system, such as
steroid-based pharmaceuticals, hormones, and anti-inflammatory agents.

- Drinking beverages such as La Pacho (also called pau d' arco or
taheebo) tea, brewed from the inner bark of the Brazilian la pacho
tree.

- Addition of nutritional supplements including calcium (1,200 mg
daily), magnesium (1,200 mg daily), zinc (60 mg daily), vitamin
C, chromium polynicotinate (400 mcg daily), B complex, biotin
(5-15 mg daily), and beta-carotene (15,000 IU daily).

- Supplements of lactobacillus acidophilus, bifiolobacterium, lactobacillus bulgaricus, and other cultures to restore the body balance of good bacteria.

- Nutritional supplementation with naturally-occurring short-
chain fatty acids such as caprylic acid for restoring normal balance of microorganisms in the colon.

In addition, a natural antiyeast dietary program is often highly
successful for treating candidiasis.

The Antiyeast "FAVER" Diet

The Yutsis antiyeast diet consists of Fish, All meats (antibiotic-free),
Vegetables, Eggs, and Rice cakes. Therefore, it is referred to as the
FAVER diet. Only these five types of foods should be eaten for a
minimum of three weeks, or another stipulated period to be determined by the recommending physician.

The FAVER diet does not permit exposure to yeast foods or those
that provide direct nourishment for the stimulation of yeast growth.

Following the initial regimen, there is a gradual addition of food
such as pears, apples, and bananas in limited quantities. As the person's health improves, some yeast-containing foods or those with a
higher sugar/carbohydrate content are added. Foods that are high in
yeast, pickled, smoked, or high in sugar should forever be limited.

If the wholisitic physician's nature-derived therapeutic regimen fails to live up to expectations, the backup will likely be synthetic drug therapy.

Synthetic Drug Therapy

Until a few years ago, the most commonly prescribed pharmaceutical was Nystatin, an antifungal antibiotic. Nystatin has been proven to be safe, with no adverse effects or complications. The drug is nontoxic and well-tolerated by all age groups. Nevertheless, it does not completely rid the body of candida species, nor does it penetrate through the blood/brain barrier to affect the mental symptoms connected with candidiasis.

Although other pharmaceutical products such as Ketoconazole, Amphotericin B, Clotrimazole, and Griseofulvin are sometimes prescribed to combat candidiasis, many of them cause adverse side effects.

A CASE HISTORY OF A CANDIDIASIS PATIENT

In July, 1992, thirty-one-year-old Florence Dresden consulted Dr. Yutsis. Mrs. Dresden said she felt constant and devastating fatigue to the point of collapse. She had been forced to take an extended leave from her technician's job because she couldn't even manage the morning and evening commute to her place of employment.

Her other symptoms included severe pain during sexual intercouse, an impaired ability to pass urine, abdominal gas, sensations of bloating, diarrhea, severe dandruff, shingles, recurrent inflammations of the nose, continuous bronchitis, earaches, fluid running from her ear canals, and easy bruising. In addition, she reported having a vaginal infection for three months before her current consultation.

After conducting laboratory examinations and putting Mrs. Dresden through the diagnostic survey, Dr. Yutsis concluded that her symptoms were the result of candidiasis. Using the natural remedies described earlier, he proceeded to cure her of the infection. Today, Mrs. Dresden is no longer troubled by either candidiasis or any of the symptoms of the Downhill Syndrome.

THE CANDIDIASIS/CFIDS CONNECTION

In 1989, Carol Jessop, M.D., presented an impressive analysis of 1,100 of her CFIDS patients to the First International Conference on Chronic Fatigue Syndrome. About 80 percent of these patients, whom she had treated for more than nine years, had received repeated courses of antibiotics for the management of acne, urinary tract infections, bronchitis, and upper respiratory infections. In addition, a majority of the patients had reported experiencing cravings for sugar and alcohol.

Following a three- to twelve-month period of treatment with the anti-fungal medication Ketaconazole and a yeast-free and sugar-free diet, 84 percent of these patients showed significant improvement. Their fatigue was eliminated, along with many of their symptoms.

Since this anti-fungal medication was at least partially responsible for the success of her patients, Dr. Jessop concluded that an infection with a candida species must be a predominant factor in the development of the symptoms of CFIDS.

12.

DENTAL AMALGAM TOXICITY

malgam is the alloy of mercury, mixed with silver and variable amounts of other metals, that is used as a dental filling. Ever since its introduction by the American Society of Dental Surgeons (ASDS) in 1840, it has been the subject of controversy. That's because the mercury is toxic and has the potential to trigger autoimmune and carcinogenic responses from the body. Unquestionably, having amalgam dental fillings is dangerous.

Recognizing this situation, Sweden has declared mercury-containing amalgam to be an environmental hazard and, in 1992, permanently banned its use by dentists. But in the United States, mercury is packed by conventional dentists into more than four-fifths of all cavities. Reports of the deleterious effects of mercury toxicity, however, along with its association with CFIDS, continue to mount. This chapter details the dangers of mercury poisoning and discusses how this condition plays an important role in CFIDS.

SIGNS AND SYMPTOMS OF MERCURY POISONING

The signs and symptoms of mercury poisoning include persistent overall fatigue, weakness, drowsiness, adverse alterations of vision, heart palpitations, breathing troubles, headache, chills, dizziness, anxiety, depression, and nervousness. In addition, victims frequently suffer from bad breath, metallic taste, allergies, various urinary problems such as pain on urination, anemia, gastrointestinal disturbances, arthritis-like joint pain and inflammation, skin eruptions, and other conditions whose causes have been erroneously labeled by some health-care professionals as "psychosomatic."

Scientific studies show that there is a definite correlation between many of these symptoms and dental amalgam fillings. In one study, done at the University of Calgary, researchers found that the level of mercury after chewing is fifteen times greater in people with silver amalgam fillings than in people who do not have such fillings. They wrote: "Our laboratory findings in this investigation are at variance with anecdotal opinion of the dental profession that amalgam tooth fillings are safe. . . From our results we conclude that dental amalgams can be a major source of chronic mercury exposure."

During a workshop on the Biocompatibility of Metals in Dentistry in 1984, Hal A. Huggins, D.D.S., presented statistics that suggest that "mercury may affect the formation of T-lymphocytes" in a negative way. The immune system requires formation of the T-lymphocytes on an ongoing basis.

THE CFIDS/DENTAL AMALGAM CONNECTION

If the list of mercury toxicity symptoms sounds familiar, it should. There is a startling similarity between those symptoms and those of CFIDS. And there are surprising stories of people who have been cured of their symptoms when their mercury amalgams were removed.

For example, Dr. Huggins reported a case of a Florida woman who had been suffering from debilitating fatigue, chronic EBV, bladder infections, food allergies, and other familiar symptoms. When Dr. Huggins removed the amalgam from a tooth that had undergone root canal, her Downhill Syndrome symptoms disappeared.

The story of Dr. Jaro Pleva further demonstrates the magnitude of the poisoning.

AN AMALGAM TOXICITY VICTIM

From the time he was twenty, most of Jaro Pleva's teeth had their cavities repaired with dental amalgam fillings. In 1963, a gold bridge was placed in the left side of his lower jaw to replace two missing teeth. In 1976, when one of the supporting teeth for this bridge needed treatment, the hole in the tooth was temporarily filled with amalgam through an opening drilled in the gold. The final treatment was delayed for a year and then the tooth was again filled with mercury amalgam.

After this dental work, he started suffering from migraines. Then, a few months after his final dental implantation in 1977, Pleva began having more symptoms, especially irregular heartbeats. Next, he developed eye problems, but an ophthalmologist who found bleeding in the retina prescribed no treatment.

A few months later, he began to feel pain in his chest, which forced him to seek medical help. An electrocardiogram showed no heart problems, and he was given no diagnosis.

Still more symptoms developed. He suffered from deep fatigue, depression, anxiety, repeated heart palpitations, chest pain, dim vision and other retinal troubles, dizziness, joint pains, "pins and needles" sensations in the armpits and groins, an odd pulling of the lower jaw toward his collarbone, muscle weakness, skin eruptions, bleeding gums, and a pervasive metallic taste in his mouth.

Since he was a scientist, he decided to evaluate his health problems from a scientific angle, and began to wonder about his dental fillings. He noticed that the surface of the amalgam filling within the gold bridge had become black and corroded. As a corrosion expert, he was aware that the amalgam was dissolving and that the metal had ionized.

He consulted with a wholistic dentist, who removed the amalgam that was in contact with his gold bridge and substituted a plastic filling. After about three weeks, the stinging sensations in his armpits and groin disappeared, as did his skin problems. Many of the other symptoms began to diminish, but they did not disappear.

Using a scanning electron microscope with diagnostic X-ray capability, Pleva analyzed his own and other people's amalgam fillings. He observed that tooth surfaces near fillings were largely black from corrosion, the process whereby mercury and other components turn toxic.

By 1981, three years after elimination of the amalgam filling and after a great deal of study, he decided to remove all of his amalgam fillings. The results were startling. When the fillings opposite the gold bridge were removed, his migraines disappeared, followed by the chronic fatigue and other symptoms. Since he had made no other changes to his lifestyle or diet, he attributed his newfound health to the elimination of the poisons from his amalgams.

HOW MERCURY TURNS TOXIC

Mercury possesses a high chemical reactivity. In the mouth, it combines with a carbon-hydrogen compound to produce methyl mercury, which is 100 times more toxic than elemental mercury. The methyl mercury can be absorbed by the body in three ways:

1. Inhalation of mercury vapor and absorption into the lungs.

   Numerous studies show that there are considerable amounts of mercury in the respired air of people who are undergoing the dental cavity-filling process, as well as from people with amalgam fillings already in place. Another study showed that mercury levels in exhaled air were proportional to the number of fillings.

2. Oxidation of mercury and gastrointestinal tract absorption.

   All soluble mercury compounds turn into mercuric ions in the intestine. This reaction leads to absorption through the mucous tissues, so the poison is ultimately transported to every cell in the body.

3. Absorption of mercuric ions through the teeth.

   Ionized mercury is absorbed by tissues and nerves beneath fillings and root canals. The mercury is then transported through the central nervous system.

HOW TO DIAGNOSE MERCURY POISONING

If you are among the 98 percent of American who have amalgams packed into your dental cavities, you should have them removed, even if you do not experience any of the symptoms listed in the forthcoming questionnaire.

To tell if you suffer from amalgam poisoning, take the "Mercury/Toxic Metal Sensitivity Questionnaire" shown in the inset on page 89. The questionnaire was created by Keith W. Sehnert, M.D., a private-practice wholistic physician in Minneapolis, Minnesota; Gary Jacobson, D.D.S., a wholistic dentist and founder of the Airport Dental clinic located near the Minneapolis-St. Paul International Airport; and Kip Sullivan, J.D., research director for an organization located in St. Paul.

Mercury/Toxic Metal Sensitivity Questionnaire

If you have mercury amalgam fillings in your teeth and answer positively to five or more of the following questions, you should be alerted to the likelihood that you are suffering from amalgam poisoning.

1. Have you had sore gums (gingivitis) often over the years?

2. Have you had mental symptoms such as confusion or forgetfulness?

3. Has severe depression been a frequent problem?

4. Have you had ringing in the ears (tinnitus)?

5. Have you suffered from temporal mandibular joint problems?

6. Have you had unusual shakiness (tremors) of your hands or arms or twitching of other muscles?

7. Do you have "brown spots" or "age spots"?

8. Have you tended to have more colds, flu, and other infectious diseases than normal?

9. Have you had food allergies or intolerances?

10. Do you have numbness or burning sensations in your mouth or gums?

11. Do you have numbness or unexplained tingling in your arms or legs?

12. Have you developed difficulty in walking?

13. Do you have ten or more "silver" dental fillings?

14. Do you often have a metallic taste in your mouth?

15. Have you ever worked as a painter, in manufacturing/chemical or pesticide/fungicide factories (fungicides with methyl mercury ingredients), or in pulp/paper mills that used mercury?

16. Have you worked as a dentist, hygienist, or dental assistant?

17. Have you ever had yeast infections?

18. Do you have chronic bad breath or white tongue (thrush)?

19. Have you frequently had low temperatures below 97.4°F?

20. Do you have problems with constipation?

21. Do you have heart irregularities or rapid pulse (tachycardia)?

22. Do you have unexplained arthritis in various joints?

23. Is it common for you to have a lot of mucus in your stools?

24. Do you have unidentified chest pains even after EKGs, X-rays, and heart studies are normal?

25. Is your sleep poor, or do you have frequent insomnia?

26. Have you had frequent kidney infections, or do you have significant kidney problems?

27. Are you extremely fatigued much of the time and never seem to have enough energy?

28. Do you suffer from irritability or notice any dramatic changes in your behavior?

29. Are you taking antidepressants now, or have you been in the past?

After using this questionnaire with almost 300 people, the researchers found it was an accurate diagnostic tool. People who answer "yes" to five or more of the thirty questions should be referred to wholistic dentists with special knowledge of mercury amalgam removal.

HOW TO HAVE YOUR DENTAL AMALGAMS REMOVED

It is essential that all patients engage in a mercury detoxification program before replacing their dental amalgam fillings, because mercury released into the body during amalgam replacement may seriously aggravate the condition.

There are two procedures to choose from: 1) an IV vitamin C mercury detox program, and 2) a series of IV chelation therapies using ethylene diamine tetraacetic acid (EDTA).

In addition, patients should undergo a supplemental regimen with certain vitamins and minerals before, during, and several months after the filling replacements. These nutritional supplements condition the cell membrane to enable the stored mercury to be excreted from the cells and to allow an increased amount of oxygen to get into the cells.

SUBSTITUTES FOR MERCURY AMALGAM DENTAL FILLINGS

Wholistic dentists use a variety of nontoxic materials as mercury substitutes. These include white composite resin filling material, dental gold alloy (mixed with palladium, copper, or cobalt), enamel and dentin bonding composites, which insulate and protect the tooth's pulp against temperature changes, plastic resins, mercury-free amalgam, silver, and porcelain.

Glass ionomer materials are favored by dentists who have encountered post-operative sensitivity among their patients to plastic resins. A few have turned to the nearly pure silver fillings, but most fear that the patient could risk toxicity to silver.

HOW REMOVING MERCURY AMALGAMS WILL HELP ALLEVIATE THE SYMPTOMS OF CFIDS

There are generally two types of treatment results:

1. Removal of the amalgam brings almost complete resolution of CFIDS symptoms.

2. Removal of the amalgam, in combination with natural anti-viral therapy, an anti-yeast regimen, and correction of MID, results in a near or total resolution of symptoms.

There are other interesting signs that point to the connection between CFIDS and amalgam fillings. While analyzing serum chemistry, Dr. Huggins found an interesting pattern of abberations in the metabolism of glucose, cholesterol, and triglycerides. Mercury, by altering sulfur-binding sites, can cause hyperglycemia, or the elevation of blood sugar levels. Subsequent elevation in blood-insulin levels results in decreased glucose levels, or hypoglycemia. Triglyceride levels have been found to be 200 to 300 percent higher in patients with mercury toxicity.

By comparison, the same three metabolic abberations are seen as parameters of MID, which we have seen is one of the cofactors of CFIDS. Thus, there is a clear connection between dental amalgam toxicity, MID, and CFIDS.

Dr. Huggins also explored the dental amalgam toxicity-candidiasis connection, and found that the body's ability to cope with the yeast is significantly diminished in patients with mercury toxicity. Moreover, when amalgams are removed, candidiasis improves.

How does this occur? Byproducts of methylation of mercury and metabolic reaction caused by candida overgrowth create an alternative pathway for candida. This alternative pathway bypasses the regular route that can be blocked by anti-fungal medications, thereby allowing candida to trick the drugs.

As you can see, mercury toxicity from dental amalgams is interrelated with at least two cofactors of CFIDS, confirming the multifactorial nature of the Downhill Syndrome.

13.

HOW HEAVY METALS AND CHEMICALS POISON THE BODY

Thirty-five years ago, Rachel Carson's book, *Silent Spring*, first warned society against the environmental and health damage caused by chemicals absorbed into the earth. Her disclosures initiated the modern environmental movement. Unfortunately, the movement has had only limited influence and, as we approach the twenty-first century, all of us continue to be adversely affected by pollution.

Pesticides, insecticides, herbicides, industrial wastes, hazardous wastes, heavy metals, and other chemical residues found in the body are now causing people to experience increasingly dangerous diseases, including the Downhill Syndrome. They are prime factors of metabolic immunodepression, leaving the body vulnerable to other cofactors such as viruses and candida.

THE PERVASIVENESS OF CHEMICALS AND HEAVY METALS

According to documents released in 1994 under the U.S. Freedom of Information Act, no fewer than 8,055 Americans die annually simply from consuming pesticides coated on food or absorbed into it.

Because of modern industrial technology, each person living in Western industrialized countries is at least a thousand times more polluted with chemicals, toxic metals, or heavy metals than people who lived in Biblical times.

Not only is chemical and toxic-metal contamination of the human body commonplace, it is an important source of the symptoms of the Downhill Syndrome. Results of a 1993 questionnaire illustrate this connection. The questionnaire, given by the Toxic Element Research Foundation of Colorado Springs and devised by the Huggins Diagnostic Center under the supervision of Hal A. Huggins, D.D.S., was distributed to 1,320 patients who were in treatment or consultation for heavy metal toxicity.

Of the respondents, more than 50 percent complained of unexplained irritability, numbness and tingling in their extremities, unexplained chronic fatigue, bloating, regular constipation, tremors or shaking of hands and feet, and twitching of face muscles. A high percentage of the respondents also complained of having a frequent metallic taste in their mouths, unexplained skin eruptions, unexplained chest pains, and headaches. In other words, symptoms we have become familiar with in connection with the Downhill Syndrome.

HEAVY METALS

Toxic metals are loosely defined as those elements whose presence at certain concentrations is known to interfere with normal metabolic functions. Physicists classify a metal as "heavy" if it has a specific gravity of five or more times that of water.

Of the twenty-two known heavy metals, four (in addition to mercury, which was discussed in the previous chapter) are polluting our environment in threatening amounts: nickel, arsenic, cadmium, and lead. A fifth metal, aluminum, although not classified as "heavy" because of its weight, is dangerous enough for inclusion in this chapter.

How Heavy Metals Poison the Body

Ingestion of heavy metals destroys brain tissue and nerve cells by increasing the cells' membrane permeability. This allows nutrients to escape from the cells. These metals also inhibit the production of enzymes, which, in turn, depresses the body's chemical reactions. The result is lowered energy and a predisposition to chronic fatigue.

Common Exposures To Heavy Metals and Symptoms of Poisoning

Each of the heavy metals is found in varying industries and in different products that people are commonly exposed to. The following lists the most common sources of the heavy metals, common occupational exposures, and symptoms of poisoning.

Nickel is among the most toxic dental materials. The metal is often found in jewelry, cigarette smoke, hydrogenated fats (as a catalyst), fertilizers, and metal cooking utensils. When cooking acidic foods, nickel may be released from stainless steel pots. Symptoms of nickel poisoning include dim vision, constipation, sore throats, loss of appetite, itching, poor digestion, acute stomach pain, hoarseness, and a dry, hacking cough.

Arsenic is a common environmental contaminant. Natural concentrations of arsenic in foods are rapidly absorbed but also quickly excreted. Metabolically absorbed arsenic, on the other hand, is transported by the blood to the kidneys, liver, spleen, skin, hair, and nails, and can remain in body tissue long after it has disappeared from the blood, urine, and feces.

Common sources of arsenic are insecticide residues on fruits and vegetables, drinking water, automobile exhaust, livestock feed additives, wallpaper dye and plaster, and household detergents.

People with likely occupational exposure to arsenic include vintners, gold miners, boiler operators, canners, painters and paper hangers, bookbinders, taxidermists, tree sprayers, petroleum refinery workers, and forestry workers.

Common signs and symptoms of arsenic poisoning include headaches, drowsiness, weak muscles, brittle nails, hoarseness, pigmented spots on the body, transverse white ridges on nails, hypertension, and jaundice.

Cadmium is poisonous to every human body system, whether ingested orally or inhaled. Once absorbed, the elimination rate for cadmium is quite slow, so it is common to find low-grade toxicity, especially among people occupationally exposed to cadmium sources.

Common sources of cadmium poisoning include drinking water, processed foods, cigarette smoke, refined wheat flour, ceramics, silver polish, fungicides and pesticides, polyvinyl plastics, rubber tires, burnt motor oil, and black polyethylene (a common electrical insulator).

Occupations that expose workers to cadmium include battery manufacturing, paint manufacturing, ceramic making, fungicide manufacturing, and people who do electroplating and soldering.

Signs and symptoms of cadmium poisoning include chronic fatigue, iron-deficiency anemia, hypertension, pain in lower back and legs, emphysema, yellow coloring of teeth, pain in the sternum, and kidney stones.

Lead has been recognized as a poisonous element for at least five decades. Tolerance to this toxic element varies with several factors: age, the form of contamination, the sources from which it comes, and the composition of the diet being consumed by the affected person.

In the atmosphere, we are exposed to lead through motor vehicle exhaust, coal burners, and dust. Other common sources include drinking water, lead plumbing, bone meal, toothpaste, newsprint, paint on pencils, wine bottled with leaded caps, car batteries, tobacco, mascara, certain hair dyes, canned pet food, milk from animals grazing on lead-contaminated pastures, and vegetables grown in lead-contaminated soil.

Occupations that expose workers to lead include foundry workers, glass manufacturing, bookbinding, gold refining, battery manufacturing, artificial flower manufacturing, insecticide manufacturing, canning, dying, metal working, farming, and plumbing.

Signs and symptoms of lead toxicity include chronic fatigue, headaches, insomnia, irritability nervousness, dizziness, anxiety, muscle weakness, confusion and disorientation, abdominal pain, loss of appetite, hypertension, iron-deficiency anemia, decreased fertility in men, impairment of the adrenal gland function, and blue or black lead lines at the base of a person's teeth.

Aluminum is used in numerous products. Prolonged exposure to this nonheavy toxic metal is common, and is a source of many diseases, particularly dementia exhibited in Alzheimer's patients.

Common sources of aluminum include cooking utensils, deodorants and antiperspirants, baking powder, dust from industrial manufacturing, antacids, building construction materials, insulated cables and wiring, soil, milk products, dermatitis, burn and wound remedies, toothpaste, color additives, automotive exhaust, and various treatments for arthritis.

Welders, people in textiles, paper, glass, synthetic-leather, and aluminum abrasives manufacturing are all unduly exposed to aluminum.

Common signs and symptoms of aluminum toxicity include muscle aches, a lacelike shadowing on lung x-rays, Shaver's disease (which consists of persistent coughing, pain under the sternum, weakness, and fatigue), rickets, osteoporosis, and liver dysfunction.

CHEMICALS

A chemical pollutant is an unwanted and usually manmade substance present in the environment. The pollutant may be derived from gases contaminating the atmosphere, dust that irritates lungs, eyes, and skin, and substances that add impurities to drinking water and food.

Where Chemicals Are Found

Potentially dangerous chemicals are all around us. Here are just a few examples of their pervasiveness:

• Radioactive wastes in tanks at nuclear power facilities leak into surrounding soils. In 1992, for example, *The New York Times* reported that the multinational Kerr-McGee Corporation had sprayed thousands of acres of pastureland in eastern Oklahoma with fertilizer recycled from radioactive wastes.

• Automobile exhaust and chimney smoke from industrial plants thicken the air with smog and caustic "acid rain" chemicals.

• Unsafe packaging permits acrylonitrile, a toxic chemical, to seep into food.

• Polychlorinated biphenyls (PCBs) discharged into rivers and lakes have contaminated fish in areas previously bountiful and commercially productive.

• Pesticides dumped by unsuspecting Americans onto their lawns are causing considerable health risks to themselves and their children. The amount of pesticides—167 million pounds—that these homeowners use each year is more than farmers use to grow food for the entire country.

The Potential Dangers of These Chemicals

Numerous studies have been conducted to find out which chemicals pose the most danger and who is in greatest danger. These studies show a clear and present danger to both children and adults. The Environmental Protection Agency is conducting an ongoing investigation, the National Human Adipose Tissue Study. From this investigation, we know that the body fat in Americans is polluted with the synthetic plastic styrene, and that over 90 percent of Americans have xylene and benzene—known carcinogens—stored in their adipose tissue.

Dangers to Children

In 1988, driven by concerns about the potential vulnerability of infants and children to dietary pesticides, the U.S. Congress commissioned the National Academy of Sciences (NAS) to perform a two-year study to address "the question of whether current regulatory approaches for controlling pesticide residues in foods adequately protect children." Five years and $1.1 million later, the NAS finally released its report.

The study confirmed the worst fears of American parents. The NAS found that children differ from adults in both their susceptibility to harm from pesticide residues and in their exposure to those residues. Because children are still growing, exposure to a dangerous pesticide during the child's critical point in development "can permanently alter the structure or function of an organ system." Moreover, since children consume more calories of food per unit of body weight than do adults, and they consume far fewer types of foods than do adults, they have much greater exposure to the pesticides.

Philip J. Landrigan, M.D., of Mt. Sinai School of Medicine in New York City, who was chairman of the NAS panel that issued the report, observed that since the U.S. Department of Agriculture bases all pesticide-risk evaluations on the diet of a typical adult, there are no accurate figures available as to the average pesticide exposure for a typical child.

The Environmental Working Group (EWG), in a second report on this same issue, wrote: "The analysis suggests that more than one-third of a child's lifetime exposure to and cancer risk from some pesticides will accumulate by age five. Indeed, by his or her first birthday, the average American child's exposure to some carcinogenic pesticides will exceed the federal government's lifetime acceptable-cancer-risk threshold, calculated to result in one malignancy in every million [adult] individuals."

Risks for Adults

People find themselves under constant bombardment from both indoor and outdoor chemical contaminants. Building materials, carpets, natural gas, fuel oil, paint, cleaning supplies, deodorants, traffic exhaust, chlorine and fluoride in drinking water—these are only the beginning of a long list of pollutants that the American adult is confronted with every day.

Chemical analysis of a common carpet shows that it outgasses benzene, formaldehyde, styrene, and many other pollutants that fill twentieth-century buildings.

An Environmental Protection Agency study estimated that the total hydrocarbons in a new office was 1,100 ng/L, compared with 130ng/L for older offices. Another study, published in the Swedish *Proceedings of Indoor Air* in 1984, examined the breath air of 355 urban residents in New Jersey and found such chemicals as chloroform, trichloroethane, benzene, styrene, xylene, and carbon tetrachloride.

Commonly Used Toxic Chemicals

Which pesticides are being spead across America, and what do they do? In alphabetical order, here are just a few typical ones:

Dieldrin is a neurotoxin capable of destroying human nerve tissue. When the National Cancer Institute tested dieldrin, the tests showed that it significantly increases the incidence of liver cancers in high-dose male rats and adrenal gland cancer in low-dose female rats. It continues to be used as a spray on fruits and vegetables.

Endosulfan, a commonly applied crop pesticide, causes a high rate of early deaths in male rats and mice.

Kepone, chlorinated insecticide, is used against leaf-eating insects, ants, and cockroaches, and as a larvicide against flies. In tests conducted by the NCI, it was found to cause animal liver cancer. Its toxic effects, observed among agricultural workers exposed to it in Virginia, include chronic fatigue, weight loss, neurological impairment, abnormal liver function, skin rash, and reproductive failure.

Kepone has been broadly administered as a spray on crops in Latin America, Africa, and Europe. In tropical areas, including Puerto Rico, it is applied as a control of the banana-root borer. Livestock which forage on Kepone-treated land or fish taken in waters polluted by runoff from the land, cause human exposure and contamination when such livestock or fish are eaten.

Malathion, another crop insecticide, causes relatively quick death in laboratory animals.

Maleic Hydrazide, an herbicide, is applied to domestic potatoes and onions to prevent sprouting after harvest. It is highly toxic to humans, and has produced central nervous system disturbances and liver damage in experimental animals.

Mirex, a white and odorless crystal derived from benzene, has been banned in the United States. Yet, Americans get their share of the pollutant when they purchase foods grown in Latin America.

THE CFIDS/TOXIC CHEMICAL/
HEAVY METAL CONNECTION

Pesticides, insecticides, herbicides, manufacturing wastes, hazardous wastes, other chemical residues, and toxic metals found in the body are now causing vast numbers of people to experience increasingly worsening pathological symptoms. Every one of these substances is immunodepressive, thereby leaving the body vulnerable to viruses, candida, and other contributors to the Downhill Syndrome.

ARE LAWS CLEANING UP OUR EXPOSURE?

In 1994, the Clinton administration responded to the pesticide problem by issuing a "pesticide reform proposal" to eliminate a 1958 law banning all carcinogenic pesticides found in processed foods. President Clinton proposed replacing that law with a "negligible risk" policy, which only permits pesticides that cause no more than a "negligible risk" to human health.

"The Clinton administration's pesticide proposal is an attempt to sugarcoat the bitter fact that agrichemicals are causing cancer," says Michael Colby, director of Food & Water, Incorporated, the Vermont-based nonprofit consumer organization that works to keep our environment pure and clean. "It takes away a law that could prevent cancer, and replaces it with a law that manages cancer."

Meanwhile, agricultural pesticide use continues to rise. It's up by 200 percent during the last nineteen years, and it's contaminating groundwater in 46 percent of all U.S. counties.

In addition, under present laws, manufacturers may increase the amount of pollutants containing heavy metals they emit into the air by up to 490,000 pounds a year without any public knowledge.

HOW TO AVOID POLLUTANTS

Although people cannot avoid exposure to the chemicals and heavy metals that pervade the air, water, and food, there are some things people can do to improve their physical environment and their health:

- Replace gas ranges with electric ones, for people who are extremely sensitive to natural gas.

- Quit smoking.

- Get rid of whatever is not absolutely necessary to your home janitorial supplies, including paints, solvents, and anything containing synthetic chemicals. Detergents should be transferred to glass bottles with tight-fitting caps.

- Examine your heating system, which can harbor pollutants that present risks for CFIDS patients.

- Buy cars with leather upholstery, automatic window openers, and natural-fiber carpeting.

- Avoid plastics whenever possible. Replace plastic shades with ones made from glass, metal, and natural fabrics; replace plastic bowls and dishes with ones that are ceramic, glass, or wood. Use glass or metal containers instead of plastic ones.

- Replace synthetic carpeting with natural-fiber carpeting, or just keep wood floors.

14.

HOW TO ELIMINATE HEAVY METALS AND CHEMICAL POLLUTANTS FROM YOUR BODY

Although we cannot avoid all the chemicals and pesticides around us, there are ways to eliminate these substances from our bodies. We can start by aiming for an organic diet. In addition, there are other diet plans and therapies that have proven to be effective.

BENEFITS OF ORGANIC FOODS

In a two-year study of produce in the Chicago area, nutritionist Bob L. Smith found that organically produced apples, pears, potatoes, corn, whole wheat flour, and wheat berries possessed a much greater nutrient content than any commercial grades. The Smith study indicated that there is a great difference in essential mineral content between organic and commercial potatoes, wheat, and corn, three staples of the American diet, particularly in the elderly. Moreover, the organically grown foods were lower in toxic mineral content. As to why previous researchers found little difference in mineral content between organic and commercial produce, Smith points out that most other studies examined dry-ash concentration of foods, and were designed more for the food producer than the consumer. He states that most of the previous studies did not address the critical variable of post-harvest handling, which can affect the mineral content.

Although it is difficult, if not impossible, to go on a diet composed solely of organic produce, try to incorporate as much organic food into your diet as possible. Our advice is to eat an organic diet high in fresh, raw produce and supplement the diet with extra nutrients that are involved in the detoxification of pesticides, including magnesium, zinc, molybdenum, selenium, all major antioxidants, and digestive aids.

THE HUBBARD METHOD OF DETOXIFICATION

At a 1994 conference conducted by the American College for Advancement in Medicine, Megan G. Shields, M.D., presented information about the L. Ron Hubbard method of physiological detoxification. Dr. Shields, who is associated with the Shaw Health Center in Los Angeles, California, documented the Hubbard method's effectiveness in reducing adipose (body fat) levels of contaminants and pollutants such as PBB's, PCB's, PCP's, THC's, DDT's, dibenzodioxins, dibenzofurans, and pesticides. Using the Hubbard method of purification, Dr. Shields has seen clinical improvement in the signs and symptoms of the Downhill Syndrome.

In her discussion, Dr. Shields said: "There is ample evidence that these substances mobilize from deep stores to cause a variety of mental and physical effects at even low levels. This is the key—*low levels*. Almost every patient I have ever treated for low-level toxicity has at one time or another been told [erroneously] by a physician that his or her symptoms could not possibly be caused by chemical or drug toxicity because there was no evidence of an acute, toxic dose of the substance in question."

Low-level toxicity, said Dr. Shields, means that *"none* of these toxic chemicals is natural and there should be *none* in the human body. Giving a 'normal' or 'reference' range for a toxic chemical is a lie, a contradiction."

The writer, philosopher, and humanitarian L. Ron Hubbard developed a program to reduce the adverse effects of drugs and pollutants. Since its introduction in 1979, at least 100,000 people worldwide have undergone this treatment.

In this treatment, the patient is given a precisely determined dose of niacin (vitamin B_3). Because time-release (sustained-release) niacin is associated with liver dysfunction, the dose starts at 100 mg of immediate-release—*not* sustained-release—niacin.

The dose is gradually increased until doses of up to 5,000 mg are taken without any noticeable effect. After taking the niacin, the patient must engage in aerobic exercise for up to thirty minutes to enhance circulation of the niacin and to mobilize the toxins to be excreted by the body.

Next, for up to five hours daily, sweating is forced by use of wet or dry intermittent sauna treatment. The sauna must be at a temperature ranging between 140° F and 180° F and very well ventilated.

Simultaneously, polyunsaturated, cold-pressed oils are applied to the patient topically in order to block recirculation of toxins that are being excreted through the skin.

In addition, to reduce the risk of increasing the toxicity of persistent chemicals such as PBB, the patient is given increased quantities of supplemental nutrients.

On average, this treatment is given for twenty-five days. The majority of patients show significant improvement at the end of treatment. Dr. Shields has reported that her patients had diminishing fatigue, headaches, and allergies, and improvement in insomnia, constipation, muscle pain and weakness, confusion, and disorientation.

THE USE OF CHELATION THERAPY
TO ELIMINATE TOXIC METALS AND CHEMICALS

Particular amino acids, antioxidants, coenzymes, and other nutrients are able to pull heavy metals and toxic chemicals out of human tissues. These beneficial substances detoxify the body and brain so that symptoms of the Downhill Syndrome are minimized. The process by which this is done is called chelation therapy, which, as we've seen in other chapters, can be used to help rid the body of other foreign substances as well.

Chelation therapy is the process by which the ions of pollutants floating in the bloodstream or other tissue fluids are captured and bonded into ringed structures by EDTA, a synthetic amino acid. It escorts undesirable toxins out through the kidneys, our usual waste-disposal system. One major advantage of this chelating procedure is that it appears to "turn on" the body repair mechanisms, leading to softening of abnormally hardened blood vessel walls. It even removes atherosclerotic plaque, the "fatty rust" that blocks arteries and leads to heart attacks, strokes, or gangrene.

There are two kinds of chelation therapy: oral and intravenous.

Oral Chelation Therapy

Oral chelation therapy involves the swallowing of specific nutrients to aid cellular detoxification of heavy metals and other pollutants. The oral chelating agents include antioxidant nutrients, pharmaceuticals, food substances, dietary supplements, homeopathic remedies, nutritional formulations, and herbs. These agents displace toxic substances in the cells by reestablishing appropriate enzymatic interrelations and neutralizing free-radical activity.

There is a wide variety of oral chelating agents, with magnesium leading the list. Magnesium works with enzymes to break down sugar stored in the liver, thereby changing the sugar from glycogen to glucose and aiding proper pH balance. In addition, it protects against kidney stones, and protects the arterial lining from stress or changes triggered by sudden blood pressure swings.

Other oral chelating agents include:

Bioflavonoids, extracted from colored food substances in fruits and vegetables, act synergistically with vitamin C to protect and preserve the "infrastructures" of the capillary beds, promote circulation, stimulate bile production, and lower cholesterol levels.

Choline, a neurotransmitter substance of the brain that transports impulses across synapses to other nerves. Acetylcholine is a chemical substance that allows messages to travel from one nerve to another. Toxic metals alter the enzymes involved in acetylcholine metabolism. Choline supplementation reestablishes appropriate enzymatic interrelations. In addition, choline helps the liver to avoid fatty buildup and remove dissolved plaque substances.

Kelp, a seaweed that is rich in vitamins, minerals, and a number of trace elements, protects against the effects of radiation and heavy-metal toxicity.

Pantothenic acid, composed of pantoic acid and beta-alanine, is needed by every cell of the body. Known as Vitamin B_5, pantothenic acid participates in the production of the adrenal hormones and the formation of antibodies. It is essential for normal functioning of the gastrointestinal tract.

Intravenous Chelation Therapy

Intravenous (IV) chelation therapy is a safe, effective, comfortable, and relatively inexpensive treatment to detoxify tissue cells and restore blood flow. During this process, the chelating agent EDTA is injected into the body; it captures ions of minerals floating in the bloodstream or other tissue fluids and bonds them into ringed structures. The ions and the EDTA are eventually eliminated through the usual waste-disposal systems, the kidneys or the bowel.

EDTA removes undesirable metals such as lead, mercury, cadmium, iron, aluminum, and arsenic. It also normalizes the distribution of most metallic elements in the body, and improves the metabolism of calcium and cholesterol by eliminating metallic catalysts that cause damage to cell membranes.

The usual duration for the IV chelation therapy is a four-hour period twice weekly for fifteen to twenty weeks. Monthly sessions are recommended for one or two years. The process, which has been administered to about 28 million people worldwide, is absolutely safe. After the therapy, patients routinely report the reduction or disappearance of their symptoms.

Comparison of pre- and post-therapy diagnostic tests provide objective evidence of the chelation treatment's effectiveness. A 1989 study reported that "88 percent of the patients receiving chelation therapy showed improvement in cerebrovascular blood flow." In another study, 90 percent of 2,870 patients treated with chelation therapy demonstrated marked improvement of their symptoms.

These therapies help diminish the accumulation of toxic heavy metals and chemicals in the body. They are safe and effective methods for making it easier for Downhill Syndrome patients to recover.

15.

DISEASE SYMPTOMS FROM ALLERGIES

M edical science has come to recognize that the many-symptom disorder of environmental illness (EI) arises from immune deficiency in sensitive people. The disorder is brought on by exposure to common chemicals and foods that the immune systems of hypersensitive people are unable to assimilate.

In various forms, allergies are always present in people who suffer from CFIDS. When family physician David Bell of Lyndonville, New York, who was discussed in Chapter One, was searching for the cause of the CFIDS symptoms he saw in his patients, the common thread among them was a history of allergies. It is important for people suffering from the symptoms of CFIDS to understand the nature of allergies, the types of allergies that can provoke the symptoms, and some of the treatments that can alleviate many of the symptoms.

DEFINING ALLERGY

Although it is a common term, people often find it difficult to give a precise definition of "allergy." An allergy is a condition in which one person reacts adversely to substances that usually don't bother other people. A more extensive definition is given by Doris J. Rapp, M.D., F.A.A.A., F.A.A.P., Clinical Assistant Professor of Pediatrics at the State University of New York at Buffalo:

"An allergy is an abnormal response to a food, drug, or something in our environment that usually does not cause symptoms in most people. We do not know exactly why some persons develop an abnormal response, for example, to ragweed pollen or to fish, while others do not. At least 10 percent to 20 percent of the population have some manifestation of allergy at some time in their lives. Allergies can begin at any age. Substances that cause allergies are called allergens or antigens.

HOW ALLERGIES SHOW UP IN CFIDS PATIENTS

Those who suffer from adverse body responses to common items, such as gas from the kitchen range, supermarket food additives, or natural substances in foods such as corn, wheat, soy, eggs, coffee, and beef also suffer from chronic fatigue and other symptoms until the true cause of their problems is discovered.

Take the case of a bus driver who became a patient of clinical ecologist Marshall Mandell, M.D., Medical Director of the Alan Mandell Center for Bio-Ecologic Diseases in Norwalk, Connecticut. The patient had been considered to be "just plain lazy" by his relatives. When Dr. Mandell discovered that the patient was having an allergic reaction to milk, the man's lethargy was alleviated simply by avoiding milk and milk products.

In another case, a homemaker was incorrectly diagnosed as hypoglycemic. But her Downhill Syndrome symptoms were actually caused by fumes from her gas stove. The solution to her CFIDS was the installation of an electric line into her kitchen so she could cook on electric burners rather than gas ones.

Here are the symptoms of allergy that appear in CFIDS patients:

1. There are five symptoms that come and go. They include:
   - Swelling of different body parts
   - Heavy sweating, unrelated to exercise
   - Chronic fatigue that does not go away
   - Bouts of racing pulse (tachycardia)
   - Marked fluctuation of weight (up or down).

2. Evidence of food addiction—eating the same things over and over.

3. Headache, sinusitis, asthma.

4. Various typical allergic symptoms show themselves in the:

Head:	Nasal catarrh and hay fever
	Giddiness
	Mouth ulcers
	Halitosis
	Headache
	Migraine
Chest:	Asthmatic wheezing
	Tachycardia (racing pulse)
Abdomen:	Bloating after eating
	Irritable bowel
	Peptic ulcer
	Regional ileitis
	Bowel cramps
Genito-urinary:	Frequent urination
	Cystitis without infection
	Impotence
	Lack of libido
	Menstrual disorders
Musculoskeletal:	Aching muscles
	Aching joints
Skin:	Hives (urticaria)
	Itchy rashes
Mental:	Panic attacks
	Chronic anxiety
	Depression
	Persistent elation
	without cause
	Hyperactivity
	Purposeless violence
	Emotional tension
	Delusions and hallucinations
	Alcoholism
	Drug addiction

WHAT HAPPENS WHEN A FOREIGN SUBSTANCE INVADES THE BODY

As we've said, allergies are present in many people with CFIDS. To understand why, we must focus on what happens when a foreign substance enters the body. The immune system codes all foreign substances that find their way into the body's tissues as enemies, and brands them with an antigen, also known as an immunogen. (An *immunogen* is a substance that induces a detectable immune response when introduced into an animal or human; an *antigen* is a substance that can react with antibodies, whether or not the substance causes an immune response. It follows that all immunogens are also antigens, although not all antigens are immunogens). From then on, whenever a person comes in contact with the immunogen, he or she has an allergic attack.

In a person with MID, any exposure to a microorganism such as a virus, parasite, or yeast infection triggers the production of antibodies against that particular invading microorganism. The antibodies are likely to attack any other foreign invaders, whether the substance is dust, pollen, chemical, or any others we've mentioned. Perfumes, tobacco smoke, pollution, insect sprays, household detergents, and ordinary paint dried on the wall can become a problem because the immune system creates antibodies against them, transforming them into antigens or immunogens. This process occurs in people who are known as "universal reactors."

"*Universal reactors* are individuals who begin to react to an increasing number of foods and environmental agents as their energetic-molecular defenses are shattered and their general condition deteriorates precipitously," writes Majid Ali, M.D. in his book, *The Canary and Chronic Fatigue*.

"Many clinical ecologists call this a 'spreading phenomenon'— the sensitivities spread as the energetic-molecular events within their cells and tissues feed upon each other to create domino effects," continues Ali.

As potential universal reactors, Dr. Ali says, CFIDS sufferers do not tolerate biologic stressors imposed on them. For them, any allergies are huge burdens on their energy and detoxification systems.

Dr. Ali explains: "Allergy exists in almost *all* persons who suffer from chronic fatigue. I see many chronic fatigue patients who insist they do not have any allergies. A careful review of the past medical history going back to infancy almost always brings out the existence of allergic symptoms. Colicky babies are always allergic babies. Eczema of infancy is often forgotten. Tonsillectomies are almost always done for undiagnosed and unmanaged allergy. Fatigue after eating is rarely recognized as caused by food sensitivity."

CFIDS patients may demonstrate a whole range of allergies, including ones to accepted inhalant antigens (dust, feathers, animal dander, grasses, trees, molds) and controversial ones to foods and chemicals (controversial because conventional allergists do not recognize them as a possible source of allergic reaction).

TYPES OF CHEMICAL ALLERGIES

People react to a wide variety of products. Every fifth person in industrialized nations shows allergic symptoms to one or more of the following substances:

chlorinated tap water	fumes from heating systems
cigarette smoke	chemical additives in foods
hair sprays	household cleaning materials
wall paint	furniture polish and floor wax
cosmetics	deodorants and perfumes
carpeting and drapes	duplicating inks and newsprint
mothballs	chlorine bleaching agents
dry cleaning fluids	disinfectants
nail polish	materials of coal tar origin
nail polish remover	rubber cements
fabrics	freshly printed materials
detergents	food processing chemicals

Think of the potential allergic dangers derived from aerosols, which we know are toxic. To know what you're facing, all you need to do is read the warnings on product labels: "Use in a well-ventilated room," or "Do not inhale or swallow," or "Call a physician immediately."

Allergic reactions to such substances may manifest themselves as chronic fatigue, debilitating headaches, rapid heartbeat, abdominal pain, stiff neck, muscle pains, even anxiety, panic attacks, and insomnia.

FOOD ALLERGIES

Allergic illnesses may arise from the ingestion of certain foods, particularly when they are broken down through processing.

How Food Allergies Are Triggered

One trigger of allergic reactions is eating the same items over and over without natural seasonal rotation. This can cause the loss of enzymes needed to digest or metabolize those foods. When unmetabolized material enters the bloodstream, it can stress the immune system. The body responds either by triggering an antigen response or by becoming "addicted" to the components of that food.

Many food and chemical allergens have an addictive quality for patients sensitive to them. Their addictive qualities are supported by the fact that these food substances have the capacity to induce symptoms that are quickly alleviated by taking more of the allergen.

Symptoms Produced By Food Allergies

Disguised food allergies produce marked symptoms in the following anatomical areas:

- In the head: headaches (migraines), faintness, dizziness, excessive drowsiness, sleepiness, insomnia.

- In the eyes, ears, nose, and throat: runny nose, stuffy nose, postnasal drip, watery eyes, blurring of vision, ringing of the ears, earache, hearing loss, recurrent ear infections, itching ear, sore throats, chronic cough, canker sores, recurrent sinusitis.

- In the heart and lungs: palpitations, arrhythmias, rapid heart rate (tachycardia), asthma, congestion.

- In the gastrointestinal tract: nausea, vomiting, diarrhea, constipation, bloating after meals, belching, colitis, flatulence (passing gas), abdominal pains or cramps.

- On the skin: hives, rashes, eczema, dermatitis, pallor.

- In the mind: anxiety, depression, "crying jags," irritability, mental dullness, lethargy, confusion, hyperactivity, learning disabilities, poor work habits, inability to concentrate.

Favorite foods are often overlooked as sources of allergic ailments by both the doctor and the patient. The patient will say, "But I eat this every day." And every day, that patient has a headache, a skin rash, the sniffles, a bellyache, or some other discomfort. Since allergy symptoms often accompany the ingestion of the favorite foods, here is a list that identifies the allergic ailments these foods are likely to cause.

Chocolate can cause chronic fatigue, pain in the joints, generalized warmth followed by chills, dizziness, sleepiness, thickened speech, anxiety, anger, and irritability.

Corn can cause chronic fatigue, joint pains, headache, abdominal pain, mid-sternal pain, urinary urgency, inability to concentrate, irritability, depression, and prolonged crying.

Egg can cause chronic fatigue, generalized itchiness, fatigue, light-headedness, nausea, yawning, indifference, and withdrawal.

Tomato can cause chronic fatigue, severe headache radiating to the temples, and mild asthma attacks.

Milk can cause chronic fatigue, headaches, mid-sternal pain, asthma attacks, coughing, and wheezing.

Sprouts can cause chronic fatigue, headache, and moderate asthma attacks.

Malt can cause chronic fatigue, sharp headache, itchy eyes, urges to sneeze, and mild asthma attacks.

Potato can cause chronic fatigue, cold hands, pain in the shoulder, pain in the jaw, abdominal pain, sore throat, blurred vision, headache, tiredness, depression, and pallor followed by a flushing of the face.

Chicken can cause chronic fatigue, hoarse voice, chills, headache, and generalized itchiness.

Green pepper can cause chronic fatigue, stiff neck, aching shoulder, itchy eyes, itchy nose, pain in both hands, tearing of the eyes, and asthmatic wheezing.

Lettuce can cause chronic fatigue, itchy scalp, itchy ears, coughing, itchy palate, sneezing, nasal obstruction, and sore throat.

Pineapple can cause chronic fatigue, generalized itchiness, tiredness, irritability, tearing of the eyes, and nasal discharge.

Tuna can cause chronic fatigue, sneezing, coughing, itchy scalp, itchy ears, itchy eyes, painful joints, and neuralgia.

Wheat can cause chronic fatigue, dry throat, cold hands, lack of concentration, unusual hunger, jitters, fatigue, depression, abdominal cramps, joint pains and other arthritis-like symptoms.

Rye can cause chronic fatigue, nausea, perspiration, and rapid heart rate.

Citrus can cause chronic fatigue, gallbladder problems, arthritic pains, headache, nervousness, tenseness, restlessness, and lower abdominal pain.

Other Food-Related Allergies

There are two additional issues related to food allergies. One is the common problem known as the "leaky gut" syndrome, and the other is the issue of food preservatives.

The "Leaky Gut" Syndrome

It is impossible to discuss food allergies without taking a look at the issue of intestinal permeability known as the "leaky gut" syndrome. When there is inflammation that breaks down the mucosa, toxins and undigested food particles can escape through the gut wall into the bloodstream. Then, the Kupfer cells imbedded in the liver signal the rest of the body that a foreigner has entered the tissues. This, in turn, triggers immunological constituents to do battle with the unwelcome invader. If antibodies are produced, the particular food that has invaded becomes an antigen. The immune system stays in a state of alert, looking for the antigen. Thus, the allergic reaction begins.

The detoxifying enzymes of the liver also go into action, releasing free radicals that move into attack positions against the liver. Various complications related to CFIDS may result, including ulcerative colitis, arthritis, endocrine dysfunction, and debilitating fatigue. The leaky gut puts people at risk of developing the Downhill Syndrome.

Food Preservatives

Some people may be sensitive to *food preservatives* instead of the food itself—a problem that is often hard to confirm. Researchers in the division of allergy at Vanderbilt University Medical Center in

Nashville, Tennessee, have been exploring food-preservative sensitivity for nearly a dozen years. They have been trying to help people distinguish between food allergies and sensitivity to food preservatives.

"There are three categories of preservatives to which people are often sensitive," explains Samuel R. Marney, M.D., associate professor of medicine at Vanderbilt. "They are bisulfites, found in beer and wine; benzoates, found in all diet and some regular soft drinks; and parabens, found in TV dinners, other prepared foods, and some medication. We find clinically that some people develop allergic spells of flushing, itching, sudden diarrhea, and often very severe headaches."

Patients who are thought to be sensitive to food preservatives can be tested. They are given the preservative dissolved in water and kept under close observation. "We measure their vital signs before, in the midst of, and at the end of the challenge," Dr. Marney said. "The histamine in the patient's urine is also measured as an indicator that there has been a positive response."

Many people mistake a reaction to bisulfites as a food allergy to shellfish. For example, "shrimp fishermen have long dipped their catch of shrimp in a bisulfite solution to keep it fresh for market," Dr. Marney explained. "If one of these [allergic] people consumes a batch of shrimp that's been treated at the point of catch, then they are likely to have a very severe reaction. Yet the next time they eat shrimp, if it has not been treated with bisulfites, they'll have no trouble at all. These are some of the most frustrated people in the world. It leads to great frustration because the patient simply can't understand why one time he or she can eat shrimp and have these symptoms, and the next time not."

Individuals who are sensitive to food preservatives, such as parabens, can avoid many of them by eating fresh or frozen packaged foods instead of canned or bottled foods.

THE CFIDS/ALLERGY CONNECTION

In 1989, the State of New Jersey Department of Health reported: "Sufficient evidence exists to conclude that chemical sensitivity is a serious health and environmental problem. Chemical sensitivity is increasingly having significant economic consequences related to the disablement of productive members of society."

Once someone is exposed to chemicals, the following sequence of events occurs:

1. Allergies develop to minute levels of the offending chemicals. This does not affect the average person, but does traumatize the immune systems of those who are hypersensitive (the majority of CFIDS patients).

2. Symptoms are at first localized to specific body parts. They manifest themselves as upper respiratory problems such as difficulty breathing, coughing, or a runny nose.

3. As exposure continues, hypersensitivity develops to a range of environmental substances chemically unrelated to the original incident. A multichemical sensitivity develops.

4. The spreading phenomenon affects additional body parts, causing prolonged fatigue, malaise, lethargy, and generalized aches and pains.

5. Allergy symptoms deepen steadily until the patient is in a total state of fatigue.

Three factors predispose people to environmental illnesses:

1. Immune dysregulation from inherited genetic defects or chronic infection from hidden focal infections, as can occur in the teeth.

2. Inability of the liver to detoxify chemicals due to heavy toxic overload. This occurs in toll collectors on bridges, tunnels, and highways.

3. Adrenal gland exhaustion from excessive stress caused by overstimulation of the senses.

CFIDS sufferers are already burdened by viruses, MID, candida, and other cofactors. This "total load" creates the perfect opportunity for the CFIDS/allergy connection to develop.

16.

TESTS AND TREATMENTS FOR ALLERGIES

Environmental illness (EI) resulting from hypersensitivity to the products of modern chemical technology and foods is a much-neglected area of medicine. Many people suffer from symptoms of hypersensitivity to something in their surroundings, and yet have no idea of its existence. Unnecessarily, they accept discomfort, disease, and disability as part of life.

The underlying causes of allergic responses are rarely—if ever—identified correctly. This is the reason why a victim of EI, with the assistance of an open-minded health professional, must look into his or her own problem. The patient alone will reap the rewards of being released from the shackles of neurotic labels, the stigma of mental illness, difficulties of EI, limitations of physical allergy, and disabilities of being victimized by the Downhill Syndrome.

A TYPICAL CASE OF ALLERGIC PROVOCATION OF DOWNHILL SYNDROME SYMPTOMS

When she first consulted Dr. Yutsis in March 1993, Mollie Gallagher, 43, stated, "I'm always tired! I have no energy! I'm drowsy all the time, especially at 4 p.m. Yet, I can't sleep at night." She had a history of insomnia, severe depression, childhood asthma, frequent sinusitis, disabling premenstrual syndrome, cravings for sugared foods, metabolic obesity, headaches, earaches, chronic sore throat, eczema, and difficulty in breathing, with wheezing occurring when she entered moldy rooms. All these symptoms were adding up to suspicions of the Downhill Syndrome. In addition, her respiratory symptoms were increased when outdoors on windy days and aggravated by the dust raised when doing housework.

When he tested her, Dr. Yutsis discovered that Mrs. Gallagher was highly allergic to molds, grasses, trees, and sulfur drugs, among other antigens. Because the patient was allergic to a vast number of substances, Dr. Yutsis administered a series of anti-allergy injections that included pollen, yeast, molds, house dust, dust mites, epidermal mix, ragweed, pigweed, many grasses, trees, and a variety of foods including cauliflower, onion, sesame seed, coffee, string beans, chocolate, citrus fruits, and wheat.

Part of the therapy included intravenous infusions of nutrients such as vitamin C and other beneficial supplements. Mrs. Gallagher was given a yeast and sugar-free diet to follow to counteract her body's allergic responses and control her yeast overgrowth.

By September, 1993, after six months of treatment, Mrs. Gallagher had lost a total of twenty pounds, and her symptoms had vanished.

TECHNIQUES TO DIAGNOSE AND TREAT ALLERGIES

The major problem in allergy treatment today is that most conventional allergists administer drug remedies designed to gain relief of symptoms. Many treatments for symptomatic relief actually make the basic underlying cause of the problem more severe. For example, nasal sprays, which are used for decongesting the mucous membranes, work temporarily; however, they themselves irritate the mucous membranes. When the effect wears off, it leaves the membranes more irritated than before. In addition, the use of the spray causes an increased need for future medication.

The real answer to an allergic reaction is to find the basic underlying cause that makes one's body overreact to everyday substances.

There are a variety of ways to determine the source of an allergy. There are skin tests, specific ways to fast, under-the-tongue provocation, the inhalation challenge test, the radioallergosorbent test (RAST), and the cytotoxic test, among others. The simplest way to begin diagnosis is to take the Symptoms and Lifestyle Survey for Chemical Allergies shown in the inset on page 123. You can score yourself and make the determination of whether or not you manifest tendencies of an allergic person.

Symptoms and Lifestyle Survey for Chemical Allergies

There are eighteen questions in this survey of symptoms/lifestyle, which goes a long way toward helping to determine your predisposition to chemical allergies. A score of more than seven positive responses indicates that allergies are a probably cause of your Downhill Syndrome symptoms.

1. Do you suffer from any of the following diseases or symptoms:

    - Asthma?
    - Eczema?
    - Migraines?
    - Rhinitis?
    - Sinus trouble?
    - Hay fever?
    - Rose fever?
    - Chronic cough?
    - Abdominal discomfort, including irritable bowel syndrome?
    - Muscle and joint pain?
    - Rapid or irregular pulse?
    - Heart palpitations?
    - Itchy or frequent sores?
    - Sneezing spells?
    - Red or puffy eyes?
    - Sore throat or difficulty swallowing?
    - Postnasal drip or nose bleeds?
    - Fatigue?

2. Have you ever taken antibiotics for a long period of time, such as for:

    - One month?
    - Two to six months?
    - Longer than six months?

3. Do your symptoms of discomfort worsen indoors?

4. Do your symptoms improve indoors?

5. Do your symptoms flare when going from air-conditioned areas to the open air?

6. Are your symptoms worse in damp places?

7. Do you have any nasal symptoms with or without itching of the eyes while you are playing or working on the lawn or in the grass?

8. Do you have frequent itchy feelings in or over your ears, eyes, nose, throat, roof of the mouth, rectum, or between the shoulder blades?

9. Do you have adverse reactions to animals?

10. Do you develop your symptoms while dusting or sweeping?

11. Are your symptoms worse around feed mills, barns, or in certain homes?

12. Do your symptoms increase in bed about thirty minutes after retiring for the night?

13. Are your symptoms worse outdoors from 4:30 p.m. to 8:30 p.m.?

14. Are your symptoms worse in the cool evening air?

15. Are your symptoms worse at work?

16. Have you ever noticed an increase in symptoms in shopping malls, schools, cars, beauty salons, carpeting stores, hospitals, or houses of worship?

17. Do chemical products (exhaust fumes, soaps and detergents, rubber goods, polishes, floor waxes, bleaches, hairsprays, perfumes, newsprint, tobacco smoke, and other chemicals) cause symptoms described in Question 1 of this questionnaire?

18. Do you ever feel fatigued or stressed out after being exposed to something in the environment that you've touched, smelled, eaten, or drunk?

Patients provide physicians with their long list of confusing health problems and sometimes find themselves treated contemptuously by a noncomprehending traditional doctor. Subsequently, the underlying sources of their illnesses go undiagnosed.

So the first job of a health professional who practices environmental medicine—the clinical ecologist—is to cut through the confusion. These doctors use testing methods that differ from standard allergy-testing procedures used by physicians practicing conventional medicine.

Fasting to Determine Food Allergies

One of the reasons it is so difficult to determine a food allergy is that the interval between eating an offending food and the appearance of physical or mental symptoms of allergy varies from person to person, and can last from several seconds to several days. A good way to self-diagnose is to undergo a period of total fasting, eliminating all food for four, six, or eight days. A first fast should last five days. People who have fasted before can go for eight days. The foods are then replaced into the diet one by one, so you can observe if any of the old familiar symptoms develop.

Fasting Procedures

Fasting should be taken seriously and should be done under a physician's supervision. Here is the procedure to follow:

- Clear the gastrointestinal tract. To do this, you must undertake a cleansing procedure with enemas or a mild laxative after a final meal. Such cleansing should be done every day during the fast.

- Drink no less than two quarts of pure spring water daily to wash out the food and chemical residues in the body.

- Refrain from any vigorous exercise.

- Keep warm; fasting causes people to feel chilled.

- Bathe regularly, but avoid taking hot or cold baths or showers to limit exposure to extremes of temperature.

- Don't smoke or take usual medications, and don't take any vitamin or mineral nutritional supplements.

- Brush teeth with sea salt or baking soda, not toothpaste. As you fast, bad breath will disappear as your body becomes cleaner.

- Write a page of text at nine in the morning, noon, three o'clock, six in the evening, and ten at night. Compare these handwriting samples to see if the penmanship becomes clearer as each day of fasting continues. A more controlled writing style is often the result of getting offensive food components out of your body and brain.

After fasting for five days, you may begin a series of food tests to provoke symptoms to determine the foods to which you are allergic.

What To Do After Fasting

Your digestive enzymes need adequate time to get into a "working mood" after vacationing for five or more days. Therefore, when breaking the fast, eat only a small amount the first day. A physician should instruct you to eat slowly. One by one, foods are replaced into the diet, and observed closely to see if any of the old familiar symptoms develop.

To duplicate your illness, a physician may give a series of provocation tests. Test foods are prepared as an extract in minute proportions. Chemical provocateurs are prepared similarly. The extract, in a 1 to 300,000 dilution, is dropped under the tongue. A reaction indicates an allergy.

An easier way to determine food allergies without fasting is by following the Rinkel Rotary Diversified Diet (RRDD).

The Rotary Diversified Diet

Developed by Herbert John Rinkel, M.D., the RRDD is simultaneously a testing procedure and a treatment for food allergy. Some food sensitizations are transitory, so refraining from eating the specific offending food for days or weeks will permit the food's reintroduction into the diet occasionally without any abnormal reaction. Eating it repeatedly, unfortunately, is likely to reinstate the sensitivity. By trial and error, the allergic person can establish a schedule that will permit the food to be eaten at specific time intervals without ill effects.

You will be asked to rotate all categories of foods (grains and cereals, fruits, vegetables, meats or fish). On days one, five, and nine you will be asked to eat just one group of foods. On days two, six, and ten, a different group of foods will be suggested. And on days three, seven, and eleven, another food group will be consumed. This rotation includes one food from each category. You will then observe whether you develop any symptoms to a specific food.

Diagnostic Testing for Leaky Gut

Nutritional consultant Jeffrey Bland, Ph.D., Chief Executive Officer of HealthComm, Inc. in Gig Harbor, Washington, has reported an accurate test to identify leaky gut:

"The patient consumes two carbohydrate sources, lactulose and mannitol. In five hours, the urine is collected to determine if (or how much) the body has metabolized the carbohydrates. What makes these carbohydrates diagnostic is that they are not normally metabolized by the body—they should pass right through the gut, exiting the body via the feces. So if they appear in the urine, it demonstrates that they 'leaked' through the gut wall, confirming the diagnosis of leaky gut."

Once diagnosis has been made, he says, "The increased liver burden increases the release of oxidants resulting from the activation of the detoxifying enzymes. Those oxidants, if not caught and quenched with anti-oxidants, can cause damage. The primary anti-oxidants are vitamins C and E." There are other anti-oxidant free-radical quenchers that work well, including glutathione peroxidase, catalase, superoxide dismutase, methione reductase, niacin, L-carnitine, and coenzyme Q_{10}.

Cytotoxic Tests for Food and Chemical Allergies

Cytotoxic testing shows any damage to the white blood cells and other blood components caused by foods or chemicals. During the cytotoxic test, a technician microscopically observes the interaction of certain food extracts with the patient's blood components.

Intradermal Techniques to Diagnose and Treat Allergies

Two effective methods for both testing and treatment of allergies are called intradermal techniques. The first, known as "Serial Dilution Endpoint Titration" (SDET), is similar to traditional skin testing and is useful in testing inhalants. In this test, however, antigens are diluted serially and injected under the skin one dilution at a time. Depending on the size of the first reaction, either weaker or stronger dilutions are administered until the end-point—the weakest dilution that produces a positive skin reaction—is found. The end-point determines an accurate treatment dose for allergy injections.

For food and chemical testing, a different type of intradermal technique, the Provocative Neutralization Test, is employed. After the baseline symptoms are established, an antigen is injected under the skin. The skin reaction is measured and symptoms are noted to identify an allergic reaction. A progressively weaker dilution at a 1:5 ratio is injected every ten minutes until the allergy symptoms appear.

These tests give the physician a reliable guide for immunotherapy, or allergy injections. For inhalant allergies (dust, molds, pollen, feathers), small amounts of antigens based on the end-point dilutions are given to produce antibodies that block the allergic reactions. For food allergies, food extracts are usually given every four days when the particular food is in rotation. Chemical extracts are usually administered sublingually (under the tongue), although intradermal injections are also given.

Additional relief is offered by the following nutritional formulas.

Ten Immune-Boosting Nutrient Formulations To Relieve Allergy Symptoms Connected to the Downhill Syndrome

1—THE SUPER IMMUNITY FORMULA

This is a combination of vitamins, minerals, glandulars, and herbs that stimulate the immune system to act against invading microorganisms. It is useful in treating chronic fatigue, general tiredness, and physical or emotional stress caused by allergies. To be taken daily:

Pantethine	60 mg
Raw adrenal	20 mg

Vitamin C	1,200 mg
Niacinamide	60 mg
Niacin	15 mg
Bromelain	20 mg
Bioflavonoids	200 mg
Black currant seeds	500 mg
Biotin	500 mcg
Chromium (chromium chloride)	200 mg
Folic acid	800 mg
Magnesium (chelate)	300 mg
Placenta	25 mg
Vitamin B_6	20 mg
Pyridoxal-5-phosphate	1 mg
Selenium (sodium selenite)	200 mcg
Vitamin A	10,000 IU
Beta-carotene	5,000 IU
Vitamin E	200 IU
Vitamin B_{12}	300 mcg
Methionine	600 mg
Inositol	200 mg
Zinc (chelate)	30 mg
Licorice root	60 mg
Echinacea	100 mg
Garlic (odorless)	500 mg

2—THE SUPER ANTI-ALLERGY FORMULA

This is a comprehensive formulation of nutrients designed to block the release of histamines and other agents, thus relieving any allergic reactions. It is effective for both acute illness and the prevention of illness. To be taken daily:

Pantethine	50 mg
Vitamin C	1,000 mg
Bioflavonoids	200 mg
Pantothenic acid	100 mg

Echinacea	200 mg
Methionine	600 mg
Vitamin B$_6$	40 mg
Quercitin	200 mg
Catechin	100 mg
Hesperidin	100 mg
DGLE	100 mg
Molybdenum	200 mcg
Coenzyme Q$_{10}$	6 mg
Vitamin A	2,000 IU
Beta-carotene	2,000 IU
Vitamin D	400 IU
Vitamin E	400 IU
Vitamin B$_{12}$	40 mcg
Magnesium	200 mg
Potassium	35 mg

3—THE SUPER ANTI-OX FORMULA

This is a potent formulation of the most powerful free-radical scavengers. Its ingredients are protective against the harmful effects of cigarette smoke, alcohol, air and water pollution, radiation, stress, and help detoxify heavy toxic metals and drugs. The formula is beneficial in the prevention of chronic degenerative diseases including arthritis, cancer, heart disease, and allergies. To be taken daily:

Pycnogenol	12 mg
Coenzyme Q$_{10}$	5 mg
Beta-carotene	10,000 IU
Vitamin A	10,000 IU
Vitamin E	150 IU
(d-alpha tocopherol)	
Glutathione	50 mg
Selenium	100 mcg
L-Cysteine HCl	400 mg
N-Acetyl-Cysteine	200 mg
Vitamin C	1,000 mg
(calcium ascorbate)	
Zinc (zinc gluconate)	30 mg

Magnesium	100 mg
(magnesium sulfate)	
Pyridoxal-5-Phosphate	5 mg
Taurine	600 mg

4—THE SUPER DETOX FORMULA

This is an effective herbal and nutrient formulation for reducing toxic load on the liver, gall bladder, kidneys, and other organs. It not only detoxifies, but also aids in the repair and restoration of malfunctioning organs. Essential in the treatment of alcohol abuse, liver disorders, heavy metal toxicity, and the damaging effects of radiation, it offers vital components for any nutritional health program. This formula should be taken daily for one to two months, to be followed by a one-month break.

Methionine	400 mg
Choline bitartrate	100 mg
Inositol	100 mg
Dandelion root	100 mg
Silymarin	70 mg
Beet root	50 mg
Black radish	50 mg
Uva ursi	50 mg
Goldenseal root	50 mg

5—THE SUPER ANTI-CANDIDA COMPLEX

This is a combination of powerful substances that enhance bowel ecology by acting as natural antibacterial, antifungal, and antiparasitic agents. The formula, especially effective for candida overgrowth and yeast infections, is used to treat various digestive disorders as well as the autoimmune dysfunction that occurs in allergies.

Grapefruit seed extract	150 mg
Sodium caprylate	100 mg
Biotin	200 mcg
Pau d'arco	200 mg

6—THE SUPER FLORA COMPLEX

This unique formulation offers a wide spectrum of "friendly bacteria" as well as other nutrients needed for healthy functioning of the digestive system. The formula helps improve digestion by preventing the infiltration of harmful microorgansims including pathogenic bacteria and fungi. It also eliminates excessive gas, bloating, and constipation. To be taken daily:

> Complex dietary fiber
> Magnesium sulfate
> Garlic
> Taurine
> *Lactobacillus acidophilus, Lactobacillus bifidus,*
>   *Lactobacillus bulgaricus*

7—THE SUPER C PLUS FORMULA

This is a highly effective hypoallergenic vitamin C formulation that provides a wide range of health benefits, such as powerful antioxidant activity, anticancer activity, immune system support, and protection against infection, inflammation, and allergy. To be taken daily:

Vitamin C	500 mg
Quercitin	50 mg
Rutin	50 mg
Hesperidin	50 mg
Catechin	100 mg

8—THE SUPER GLUCOSE CONTROL FORMULA

This formulation provides ingredients that play essential roles in helping to stabilize variations in blood sugar levels. Beneficial to diabetics, hypoglycemics, and many others who crave sweets, the formula also reduces cardiovascular risk factors such as hypertension, HDL/LDL serum cholesterol abnormalities, and elevated triglycerides. To be taken daily:

Chromium polynicotinate	100 mcg
Manganese	20 mg
Vanadyl sulfate	10 mg

| Selenium | 30 mcg |
| Inositol nicotinate | 400 mg |

9—THE SUPER PANTETHINE FORMULA

This formulation helps lower high blood-serum cholesterol and triglycerides. By reducing the toxic effects of acetaldehyde, pantethine helps in the treatment of chronic candidiasis and alcoholism and decreases the risk of developing cardiovascular disease from tobacco smoke. The formula aids in the body's ability to grow *Lactobacillus acidophilus* and to reduce sensitivity to allergic substances, especially formaldehyde. To be taken daily:

Pantethine	150 mg
Pantothenic acid	150 mg
(d-cal pantothenate)	

10—THE SUPER Q_{10} FORMULA

This pure high-potency preparation of coenzyme Q_{10} becomes involved in the actual production of energy within body cells, especially in producing heart cell energy. Accordingly, this nutrient is used for the treatment of heart disease, high blood pressure, immune system stimulation, allergies, life extension, slowing down of the aging process, periodontal disease, and peptic ulcers. Since the natural coenzyme Q_{10} levels in the body decline with age, it should be taken as a supplement to the diet. To be taken daily:

| Coenzyme Q_{10} | 30 mg |

HOW TREATING ALLERGIES AFFECTS CFIDS PATIENTS

Elimination of the contributing factors to CFIDS usually leads to the lessening and, sometimes, to a complete disappearance of the CFIDS symptoms. The fewer contributing factors remain to be eliminated, the greater the patient's chance of recovery.

Therefore, undergoing treatment for allergic responses to food and environmental excitants goes a long way to helping Downhill Syndrome patients eliminate their varied symptoms of distress.

17.

UNDERACTIVE THYROID —ANOTHER CONTRIBUTING FACTOR

The endocrine system conditon called hypothyroidism is marked by decreased activity of the thyroid gland. People with this health problem experience weight gain, sluggishness, dryness of the skin, constipation, arthritis, slowing of the body processes, a truly burdensome chronic fatigue, and other symptoms.

At first, the condition produces no recognizable symptoms, and when they do start to become noticeable, the discomforts tend to be vague and seemingly unrelated to one another. That's why the chronic fatigue of the Downhill Syndrome may not immediately be attributed to hypothyroidism.

HOW THE THYROID GLAND WORKS

Located in front of the trachea, the thyroid gland produces the iodine-containing hormones thyroxine (T_4) and triiodothyronine (T_3). These two hormones are incorporated in the protein thyroglobulin, which is stored and released into the blood when it is needed by the body. The gland's main function is to secrete quantities of hormone adequate enough to meet the demand of the peripheral tissues and cells.

When combined with the amino acid tyrosine, the T_4 hormone is formed within thyroid tissue. Then, in order to exercise its influence, T_4 must be converted to T_3, which is more active and potent. T_3 keeps in check metabolic processes that constantly take place at the cellular and tissue levels. Together, T_4 and T_3 regulate the multitude of enzymes that control and influence all metabolic reactions, including energy usage.

The physiologies of T_4 and T_3 are interdependent and complicated. Thyroid hormone secretion depends on the amount of thyroid-stimulating hormone (TSH) released from the portion of the brain known as the adenohypophysisis. In turn, the level of TSH depends on the amount of thyrotropin-releasing hormone (TRH) released by the hypothalamus portion of the brain.

In hypothyroidism, a decrease of T_4 and T_3 in the blood signals the hypothalamus to release elevated levels of TRH to stimulate the pituitary. By increasing production of TSH, the pituitary strongly stimulates the production of T_4, attempting to bring the T_4 level to a normal condition. A person with hypothyroidism feels the symptoms reported by Dr. E. Denis Wilson, M.D., of Longwood, Florida: cold hands and feet, depression, constipation, headaches, lost sex drive, muscle weakness, poor memory, premenstrual syndrome, dry skin, and easy susceptibility to infections.

WILSON'S SYNDROME—A NONTRADITIONAL VIEW OF SLOW THYROID FUNCTION

The International College of Endocrinology estimates that 34 million men, women, and children in Canada and the United States have underactive thyroid glands. Recently, physicians have come to agree that hypothyroidism is caused by excessive emotional, mental, environmental, and physical stress (infection, food poisoning, toxic metal ingestion, and more). Such a modified form of hypothyroidism has now been alternatively labeled by the pathological condition's discoverer, E. Denis Wilson, M.D., as "Wilson's Syndrome." It is one of the most recent clinical entities found to be connected overall to the Downhill Syndrome.

Traditional endocrinologists diagnose hypothyroidism only if blood levels of the thyroid hormones are low. But these blood levels only tell part of the story. When conversion of T_4 into T_3 is impaired, the metabolism of the body's cells and tissues suffers. The thyroid slows down in spite of normal blood-hormone levels. In other words, Wilson's Syndrome represents a subclinical hypothyroidism because of normal thyroid hormone levels in the blood.

What can alert physicians to the presence of Wilson's Syndrome is a patient with body temperature that runs, on average, below normal, even when the routine thyroid blood tests show in the "normal range."

Diagnosing Wilson's Syndrome

When taken orally, the average body temperature of a healthy, resting adult is 98.6° F, and some temperature difference of 0.5° to 1° F can be considered normal. A lower temperature may be the sign of Wilson's Syndrome, or "subclinical" hypothyroidism resulting from stress. Dr. Wilson advises that a temperature lower than 98.6° F is a possible sign of hypothyroidism when it is associated with headaches, migraines, premenstrual syndrome, fluid retention, depression, dry skin, decreased memory, easy weight gain, and other difficulties.

Measuring Average Body Temperature

To determine if you are suffering from Wilson's Syndrome, first take your temperature in the following manner:

1. Shake down the oral thermometer.

2. For three consecutive days, record your oral temperature three different times during the day. You should take your temperature at the same time every day (before mealtime is good) and note it in a chart (See our example).

3. Keep the thermometer under your tongue for at least one minute in order to get an accurate oral temperature reading.

Oral Temperature Recording Chart

Date	Temperature at:	10 a.m.	1 p.m.	4 p.m.

Average Daily Temperature: _____

Average Recording of Averages: _____

If you have subnormal temperature and suffer from any of the other symptoms, your next step is to take the following questionnaire, used by physicians in the two major wholistic health organizations.

Lifestyle Survey for Wilson's Syndrome

In the "Symptoms and Lifestyle Survey for Wilson's Syndrome" are twenty questions designed to help you decide if an underactive thyroid is a cofactor of your Downhill Syndrome. This questionnaire is a short evaluative stress/distress survey which focuses on your personal glandular functioning.

Symptoms and Lifestyle Survey for Wilson's Syndrome

Answers to the questions should be "yes" or "no" and your positive responses scored. Any "yes" answer to a multi-part question (such as question one) scores the entire question as positive. More than seven positive responses indicates that hypothyroidism may be a contributing factor for the presence of symptoms and signs of the Downhill Syndrome.

1. Are you suffering from any of the following conditions:
   - Chronic fatigue?
   - Depression?
   - Deterioration of your memory?
   - Low motivation?

2. Are you suffering from low blood pressure?

3. Do you have a decreased libido (sex drive)?

4. Are you suffering from constipation or irritable bowel syndrome?

5. Do you notice an inappropriate weight gain?

6. Do you have dry skin or dry hair?

7. Do you have an elevated cholesterol level or signs of glucose intolerance (hypoglycemia or diabetes mellitus)?

8. Do you suffer from allergies?

9. Do you suffer from insomnia?

10. Do you have heat or cold intolerance (feel cold when everyone else is warm, or vice versa)?

11. Are you experiencing slow wound healing?

12. Do you notice frequent anxiety or panic attacks?

13. Do you suffer from frequent yeast infections?

14. Do you have cold hands or feet that turn blue on occasion?

15. Do you suffer from frequent skin infections or acne?

16. Do you notice lightheadedness or ringing in your ears?

17. Do you suffer from arthritis or other types of joint pains, muscular aches, or inflammation of the muscles?

18. For women only: Are you experiencing irregular menstrual periods, severe menstrual cramps, premenstrual syndrome, or fluid retention?

19. Do you notice that your basal temperature (early in the morning upon awakening) or your regular temperature (during the day) has been on the low side (from 97.0 to 98.0° F or lower)?

20. Did severe chronic or acute stress situations (such as childbirth, job or financial difficulties, divorce, surgery or accidents, family troubles, or death of a loved one) preceed any of the symptoms listed in questions 1 to 19 to which you answered "yes"?

Wilson's Syndrome/CFIDS Connection

As a result of the disease's disguise, many victims never think to consult a doctor about their slowdown and constant tiredness—at least as the difficulties relate to the thyroid gland.

Dr. Paul Yutsis analyzed the presence of low body temperature (at least 1 degree lower than 98.6° F) among the Downhill Syndrome patients in his practice. As it turned out, 40 percent of these patients had low body temperature combined with severe stress situations preceeding the onset of debilitating fatigue and associated symptoms of Wilson's Syndrome. A number of holistic professionals reported identical findings in their practices. It became obvious that another contributing factor to CFIDS was identified.

Correcting Wilson's Syndrome

Once a patient is diagnosed with Wilson's Syndrome, there are a variety of ways to treat it.

T_3 Therapy

Dr. Wilson's therapy consists of giving a compound of liothyronine mixed with hydroxypropyl methylcellulose in a two-piece, hard-shell gelatine capsule filled with powder to his patients.

Hydroxypropyl methylcellulose (HPMC), a water-soluble polymer that initially forms a gel when combined with water, is a sustained-release agent. When swallowed, the HPMC in the capsule allows water to penetrate the powder fill, causing hydration and gelation. Instead of dissolving in several minutes, the gelatine capsule will dissolve in thirty to sixty minutes, leaving a gelatinous capsule-shaped plug to dissolve slowly to control the rate of release.

The patient's body eventually brings its thyroid hormone system function into normal balance, and body temperature is brought back to the normal 98.6 ° F. At any point in the therapeutic program, the patient may experience some remarkable improvements in thyroid clinical status. Improvement may continue steadily, and, after two, four, or six weeks at the same dosage, the amount of T_3 taken by the patient may be altered slightly downward so as to allow his or her body to take over its normal endocrine function.

But there are several adverse side effects to the therapy. If the patient does not take the medicine correctly and on time, the amount of T_3 hormone in the blood serum may be affected, causing body temperature to become abnormal once again and possibly triggering some symptoms. Emotional, physical, and/or mental stress can also trigger these responses.

Reversing Wilson's Syndrome Naturally

Two-thirds of the body's required iodine is stored in the thyroid gland. Since the thyroid controls metabolism, the iodine influences this gland's functioning. An undersupply of the mineral can result in slow mental reaction, weight gain, and lack of energy, among other signs and symptoms. The recommended daily allowance for iodine, as established by the National Research Council, is 150 mcg for adults (1 mcg per kilogram of body weight) and 175 to 200 mcg for pregnant and lactating women respectively. Regularly ingesting less than this amount may bring on goiter or Wilson's Syndrome.

The best natural food sources of iodine are kelp, various seaweeds, vegetables grown in iodine-rich soil, onions, fish, all shellfish, molasses, egg yolks, parsley, apricots, dates, prunes, raw milk, cheeses, chicken, and iodized salt. Nutritional supplementation is available in multimineral and high-potency vitamin supplements in doses of 0.15 mg (150 mcg) of iodine.

In addition to iodine, there are other supplements that help reverse the symptoms of Wilson's Syndrome, as shown below.

Nutritional Supplements Recommended to Treat Wilson's Syndrome

Supplement/Essential:	L-Tyrosine (amino acid)
Suggested Dosage:	500 mg twice daily on an empty stomach.
Comments:	Low plasma levels have been associated with hypothyroidism.
Supplement/Essential:	Sea kelp
Suggested Dosage:	10 tablets daily
Comments:	Contains iodine, the basic substance of the thyroid hormone.

Supplement/Very Important:	Raw thyroid glandular (Armour Thyroid Tablets)
Suggested Dosage:	As directed by physician
Comments:	Available by prescription only. Synthetic thyroid hormones are often ineffective.
Supplement/Important:	Vitamin B complex including riboflavin (B_2) and B_{12} lozenges
Suggested Dosage:	Vitamin B complex: 100 mg with meals; B_2: 60 mg twice daily; 12 lozenges: 15 mg dissolved under the tongue three times daily on an empty stomach.
Comments:	Improves cellular oxygenation and energy. B_{12} is absorbed better in lozenge form.
Supplement/Helpful:	Brewer's yeast
Suggested Dosage:	As directed on label
Comments:	Rich in basic nutrients (B vitamins, etc.)
Supplement/Helpful:	Iron chelate or Floradix formula
Suggested Dosage:	As directed on label.
Comments:	Essential for enzyme and hemoglobin production.
Supplement/Helpful:	Unsaturated fatty acids
Suggested Dosage:	As directed on label
Comments:	For proper functioning of the thyroid gland.

Supplement/Helpful:	Vitamin A plus beta-carotene
Suggested Dosage:	15,000 IU daily
Comments:	Included in a multivitamin complex
Supplement/Helpful:	Vitamin C
Suggested Dosage:	500 mg 4 times daily
Comments:	Do not take extremely high doses since this may affect the production of the thyroid hormones.
Supplement/Helpful:	Vitamin E
Suggested Dosage:	400 IU daily
Comments:	Avoid large amounts
Supplement/Helpful:	Zinc
Suggested Dosage:	50 mg daily
Comments:	An immune system stimulant
Nutritional Addition with Herbs:	Useful herbal remedies recommended by naturopaths for correcting the metabolism of hypothyroidism are bayberry, black cohosh, and goldenseal.

When Wilson's Syndrome is reversed, a majority of Downhill Syndrome patients feel better. Simultaneously, when other contributors are taken care of (immune enhancement program is initiated, anti-candida treatment is conducted, mercury amalgams are removed, heavy metal and chemical toxicity is addressed properly, and allergies are eliminated), a dramatic improvement in the patient's condition will follow.

18.

PARASITES AS DISEASE FACTORS

I ntestinal parasites have existed since our evolution as homo sapiens, yet they have been recognized as medical entities only within the last 200 years. These protozoa, helminth worms, and bacteria may even have been a factor in Darwinian selection. And evidence shows that parasites have been found in many patients suffering from CFIDS, leading scientists to believe that parasitic infection can cause many of the familiar symptoms of the Downhill Syndrome. With the ever-growing incidence of CFIDS, physicians and health-care scientists have turned their attention to bowel ecology in their quest for understanding of immune dysfunctions.

Wholistic physicians view the intestinal tract as the ecosystem that supplies a home for indigenous microorganisms. At any time, intestinal parasites can turn into factors harmful to the health of CFIDS patients.

WHAT ARE PARASITES?

A *parasite* is any living thing that flourishes within or upon another living organism (the host). The parasite, which may spend all or only part of its existence with the host, obtains food or shelter from the host and contributes nothing to its welfare. Some parasites cause irritation and interfere with bodily functions; others destroy host tissues and release toxins into the body, thus causing disease. Examples of human parasites include viruses, fungi, protozoa, helminth worms, and bacteria.

In previous chapters, we focused on viruses and fungi. In this chapter, we focus on the intestinal parasites—protozoa, helminth worms, and bacteria—that can cause the symptoms of CFIDS.

Protozoa, micro-sized parasites, are single-cell animal organisms measuring from 1 to 10 millimeters in length that multiply within their human hosts. *Helminth worms*, much larger parasites, are multi-cellular organisms that do not multiply inside their human hosts but by producing eggs called ova or larvae. Depending how the individual parasitologist classifies the worms, there are three, four, or five classes of worms known as: (1) the *nematodes* or *round-worms*, (2) the *trematodes* or *flatworms* or *flukes*, (3) the *hookworms* (bloodsucking nematodes), and (4) the *cestodes* or *tapeworms*. And *bacteria* are microorganisms about 1 by 4 micrometers in size that come in different shapes and can cause a great number of illnesses.

THE HIGH INCIDENCE OF PARASITIC INFECTION

Most Americans assume that parasitic infections are encountered only in distant parts of the world or by people who live in impoverished rural areas. But Martin J. Lee, Ph.D., and Stephen Barrie, N.D., the owners and principal microbiologists of the Great Smokies Diagnostic Laboratory in Asheville, North Carolina, say that Americans can acquire parasitic infections without doing any traveling.

In the early part of the twentieth century, parasitic infestation was contained as government-sponsored work forces diligently went about cleaning up the environment, setting standards to clean up polluted water, and establishing public health centers. In the last five decades, however, such infestations have been on the rise, in part because of the growth of tourism and the increase in the number of immigrant food handlers from endemic areas.

The Rise Of Protozoa and Helminth Worms

The incidence of amoebiasis and giardiasis, two parasitic diseases resulting from infections by the intestinal protozoa *Entamoeba histolytica* and *Giardia lamblia*, has increased by about 8 percent over the past decade. Experts from the U.S. Department of Public Health estimate that in the New York metropolitan area alone, 25 percent of the population is infected with protozoal organisms consisting not only of *E. histolytica* and *G. lamblia* but also with *Blastocystis hominis, Dientamoeba fragilis,* and *Entamoeba coli.* These numbers are typical of most large cities in the United States.

Public-health officials say about 7 million Americans are infected with pathology-producing protozoa. Additionally, most AIDS patients are affected by amoebiasis, giardiasis, or other protozoal diseases. The Great Smokies Diagnostic Laboratory reports that 20 percent of all stool specimens examined there contain parasites, primarily protozoa.

Although we might think otherwise, statistics show that the incidence of protozoa infestation in the United States is astounding, especially compared to countries with reputations for being poorly sanitized. When Louis Parrish, M.D., of New York, analyzed 300 of his patients, he found that 65 percent of the patients with American ancestry were infested with both *Entamoeba histolytica* and *Giardia lamblia,* compared to 38 percent of his Indian-born patients and 52 percent of the Mexican-born patients.

In a recent study conducted at Johns Hopkins Hospital, 18 percent of randomly selected blood samples revealed a presence or past infection of *Giardia lamblia.* Compared to other parasites, protozoa have the most significant impact on the development of the Downhill Syndrome.

Recently, another protozoa, *Blastocystis hominis,* has attracted attention because of its unique properties. Once considered a yeast, *Blastocystis hominis* has been found in increasing numbers, and patients infected with this protozoa present symptoms such as diarrhea, abdominal pain and cramps, and nausea, among others. Since it has properties of both yeast and protozoa, *Blastocystis hominis* establishes the connection between Candida and parasites.

As for helminth worms, they are usually contracted from eating infested meat, by travel to underdeveloped countries, from pets, and from contaminated water. One or more of these helminth worm types have already invaded the intestinal tracts of at least three-fourths of the earth's population, and tens of thousands more people are being newly infected or reinfected every day.

Roundworms are especially common in tropical or subtropical areas such as Mexico, South America, Asia, and Haiti. Refugees and immigrants coming from such parasite-infested countries may be carriers, unknowingly spreading these parasites.

Undercooked fish can transmit anisakid worm larvae found in

red snapper, Pacific salmon, cod, haddock, and herring. Tapeworms that make their home in Alaskan salmon, perch, pike, pickerel, and American turbot are the largest-sized parasites that infest humans. Consuming sushi, sashimi, or other raw fish can lead to worm infestation.

Soldiers stationed overseas can harbor a variety of worms and protozoa. In 1985, a small group of Vietnam War veterans filed a class-action medical-malpractice suit against the Veterans Administration for failing to diagnose and treat a parasitic infection known as Filaria, which is caused by worms. More recently, more than half a million "Desert Storm" veterans were disqualified from donating their blood because of the incidence of the parasitic disease Leishmaniasis, spread by infested desert sand flies.

Pets play an important role in the transmission of parasites. For example, if a dog infected with heartworm is bitten by a mosquito, that insect can bite a human and transmit the worm. In her book, *Guess What Came to Dinner—Parasites and Your Health,* author Ann Louise Gittleman warns that tapeworms can be transmitted by infected fleas.

In addition, having a variety of sexual partners and engaging in anal or oral sex can lead to the spread of parasites.

As a group, however, the largest number of disseminators of parasites are workers in the restaurant industry who are not in the habit of washing their hands after defecating.

The Rise Of The Bacteria *Helicobacter Pylori*

A wide variety of digestive-tract discomforts arise because travelers become infected with protozoa, worms, bacteria, yeast, and other organisms. These parasitic invaders create inflammations in the esophagus, stomach, small intestines, colon, or rectum, causing heartburn, gastritis, peptic ulcer, diarrhea, cramps, bloating, gas, flu-like illness, or worse.

In 1978, when parasitic infections began to show a resurgence, 3 percent of all medical cases suffered from these type of symptoms. By 1996, the number of patients struck by such symptoms had doubled.

People have mistakenly attributed many of these symptoms to other causes. Two such symptoms offer a case in point. *Gastritis* is an inflammation of the lining of the stomach—the gastric mucosa.

Its symptoms include loss of appetite, nausea, vomiting, and bloating after eating. *Duodenal,* or *peptic ulcer* consists of a craterlike lesion in the mucous membrane lining of the first portion of the small intestines (the duodenum).

For decades, the medical community thought that these stomach inflammations were caused by many such factors as diet, smoking, heavy use of nonsteroidal, anti-inflammatory drugs like aspirin, physical trauma, genetic predisposition, excess amounts of stomach acid, loss of covering of the mucous membrane, and stress. The hypothesis was that excess acid secretion eventually damaged the stomach's protective lining, producing a hole or an inflammation of the tissue. This damage, in turn, was thought to produce symptoms of chronic pain and discomfort.

The accepted treatment for gastritis and peptic ulcer was any product that reduced acid flow. These products include antacids and drugs generically classified as H_2 receptor-antagonists and sold under the names Losec™, Prilosec™, Axid, Tagamet™, Zantac™, Zantac 75™, Pepcid AC™, Mylanta™, Tums®, and Maalox®. These remedies rank just behind painkillers and cold remedies in the space they take up on the nation's medicine shelf. People around the world spend nearly $7.5 billion a year on these stopgap antacid products that offer no permanent cure.

Based on research conducted by the Australian physician Barry Marshall, M.D. and his colleague, pathologist Robin Warren, M.D., we now know that the cause of these stomach problems is a bacteria known as *Helicobacter pylori*, which thrives in the stomach's highly acidic environment. Therefore, acid-altering treatments do not work because they are treating the wrong problem. Yet, doctors practicing conventional medicine are still making incorrect recommendations for gastritis and peptic ulcers.

How Doctors Made the Bacterial/Gastritis Link

The first patient ever treated for possession of the stomach organism was a fifty-four-year-old woman living in retirement with her husband near Perth, Australia. In a symposium, Dr. Marshall explained his treatment:

The woman had been experiencing chronic pains and sort of dyspeptic problems for about twenty years. When I met her, she kept being admitted to the Coronary Care Unit to rule out myocardial infarction because she was getting very atypical kinds of lower substernal epigastric episodic severe pains. We did an endoscopy, and [found] this germ and this chronic gastritis. We treated her with bismuth compound and also amoxicillin.

A month later, after we had eradicated this bacterium, her epithelial cells appeared clear, grew taller, and filled with gastric mucous. It's now being shown in a number of studies that the mucous secretion increases when we treat this problem...It appears that after you've treated Helicobacter, it's less likely that the patient will acquire the infection again because persistent immunity comes on afterwards...

Numerous clinical trials investigating the link between *H. pylori* infection with gastritis and duodenal/peptic ulcers have proven their association.

SYMPTOMS OF PARASITIC INFECTION

Referring to the two intestinal protozoa, *Entamoeba histolytica* and *Giardia lamblia*, Dr. Parrish observes: "The symptoms these organisms produce in humans are so varied, intermittent, and similar to other infections involving the immune system that only relatively recently are they being recognized as a primary cause of generalized illness."

Parasites can cause a variety of symptoms, both intestinal and extraintestinal.

Intestinal symptoms include:

- Diarrhea
- Abdominal cramps
- Flatulence and abdominal bloating
- Foul-smelling stools
- Abdominal distention
- Constipation
- Heartburn, nausea, and vomiting

General internist Leo Galand, M.D., senior research consultant for the Great Smokies Diagnostic Laboratory, has observed that parasitic organisms disturb the gastrointestinal environment, resulting in dysbiosis. In this illness, organisms that start out with low virulence induce disease by altering the immune responses of their host. Research shows that dysbiosis alone is responsible for vitamin B_{12} deficiency, irritable bowel syndrome, inflammatory bowel disease, malabsorption of food, and other medical problems.

In addition to gastrointestinal symptoms, Dr. Louis Parrish has observed extraintestinal symptoms. The specific symptoms Dr. Parrish has observed in more than thirty years of experience are:

- *Fatigue symptoms* in the form of persistent tiredness, excessive yet unrefreshing sleep, lack of motivation, and what the parasitologist calls "brownouts," the absolute urgency to close the eyes and nap at any time (including while driving).
- *Toxicity symptoms* such as lack of concentration, confusion, nightmares, musculoskeletal pains, wide swings in blood-sugar levels, and menstrual irregularities.

By now, we recognize these symptoms as those seen in patients suffering from the Downhill Syndrome.

THE PARASITE/CFIDS CONNECTION

In a study of 403 patients suffering from symptoms of CFIDS, New York parasitologist Hermann Bueno and Dr. Galland found that an astonishing 93 percent tested positive for protozoa infestation in the intestines. Of the detected protozoa, *Entamoeba histolytica* was the main invader, followed by *Giardia lamblia.*

Dr. Galland explained: "People exhibiting chronic fatigue with giardiasis is nothing new. But it is rarely picked up because the majority of people with chronic fatigue syndrome have not had a comprehensive exam to eliminate other possible causes."

The effects of protozoa on AIDS patients help explain what might happen in CFIDS patients. Researchers have demonstrated that protozoal invasion of the duodenum and upper small bowel can significantly reduce production of immunoglobulin A (IgA), the most important source of antibodies. Researchers from the University of Virginia reported that amoebas (class protozoa) can project a substance called lectin, which ruptures the immune defense cells and activates HIV from a dormant state. Freed into the bloodstream, this AIDS virus multiplies and manifests its lethal potential.

If a protozoal infection can produce such a dramatic effect on the immune function of HIV-positive patients, it may very likely produce similar effects on CFIDS patients. Dr. Galland suggests the following connection:

"Besides giardiasis, Candida and allergies make up most cases of CFS. I would estimate that all three cause some 60 percent of all cases...in particular, I find that hypersensitivity to molds, possibly related to Candida, is a frequent cause, sometimes sparked by an initial bout of giardiasis."

In addition, there is evidence that injury of the intestinal wall caused by giardia may cause reactivation of a latent Epstein-Barr virus.

Murray Susser, M.D. and Michael Rosenbaum, M.D., authors of *Solving the Puzzle of Chronic Fatigue Syndrome*, also believe that *Blastocystis hominis* may be a contributor to the Downhill Syndrome.

DIAGNOSIS OF PARASITIC INFESTATIONS

Most parasitic infections are diagnosed by means of a laboratory examination of the patient's stool specimens. Proper procedure in parasitology requires that the patient must have at least three negative specimens before the diagnosis of parasite infestation is discarded. Dr. Parrish advises that if a physician is still clinically suspicious, it is proper to test three to six more specimens.

Dr. Bueno invented a method called anoscopy, which can identify any parasites that are stuck to the intestinal wall and might have been missed by routine examination of the stool. Using this technique, he and Dr. Galland examined 403 CFIDS patients and found that an astonishing 93 percent showed parasites lodged in the intestines. These findings were confirmed with immunofluorescent studies.

Although anoscopy is the most reliable diagnostic tool, there are other tests that may be helpful to detect:

- Elevated IGE level, a sign of antigen-antibody immuno response
- Eosinophilia, consistent with excess antibodies
- Anti-amoeba antibodies.

Examination of sputum can reveal the presence of some protozoa, including *Entamoeba histolitica* and *Pneumocystis carinii,* and helminth worms. And a purged stool test—using laxatives to purge the intestines—is one of the best techniques to determine the presence of both protozoa and helminth worms.

TREATMENT OF HUMAN PARASITES

In her book, *Guess What Came to Dinner,* Ann Louise Gittleman suggests the following five steps to recover from parasitic infection.

1. Cleansing the intestinal tract by having a high fiber intake.
2. Modifying the diet.
3. Administering effective substances to eliminate the parasites.
4. Recolonizing the gastrointestinal tract with friendly bacteria.
5. Eliminating parasite risk factors from a person's lifestyle and environment to avoid reinfection.

Parasite-Eliminating Remedies

To put the third suggestion above into effect, wholistic physicians have a wide variety of medications and herbal preparations that help eliminate parasites once they have been detected.

Treatment for Protozoan Infections

Drugs:

For *Giardia lamblia*:
- Metronidazole (Flagyl) 250 mg for three to ten days.
- Quinicrine (Atabrine)
- Flurazolidone (Furoxone)

For *Entamoeba histolytica*:
- Iodoquinol (Yodoxin)
- Metronidazole (Flagyl)
- Paramomycin (Humatin)

Herbal Preparations:
(Broad-spectrum coverage)

- Artemisia annus (Parquing) one capsule, two to three times a day.
- Citrus seed extract (Paracan-144) one capsule, twice a day.
- Gozarte, Udarte, Neo-Parate (developed by Dr. Bueno) one capsule, three times a day, for 40 days.
- Padapco, Pasaloc, one capsule, three times a day, for 40 days.
- Paracitro (also effective against Candida species), one capsule, three times daily, for 40 days.

Treatment for Helminth Infections

Drugs:

For Roundworm and Hookworm:
- Mebendazole, 100 mg/kg once a day.
- Albendazole, 400 mg, one dose.

For Pinworm:
- Mebendazole, 100 mg/kg, one dose to be repeated in two weeks.
- Pyrantel pamoate, 11 mg/kg, one dose to be repeated in two weeks.

For Tapeworm:
- Praziquantel, 10-20 mg/kg, one dose.
- Niclosamide, 4 tablets chewed thoroughly.

Natural Preparations:

- Wormwood/Artemesia annua, 1/2-1/2 tsp., one to two times daily.
- Black walnut hull tincture, one drop four times a day, to be increased up to 20 drops four times a day for three months.
- Cloves, one capsule three times a day before meals, to be increased to three capsules three times a day from the third to tenth day, and then three capsules once a day for three months.

Treatment of Helicobacter Pylori

Drugs:

- Tetracycline, 500 mg, two hours before meals and at bedtime for ten days.
- Flagyl, 250 mg, with meals and at bedtime for ten days.
- Pepto-Bismol, two tablets with meals for two to three weeks.
- Biaxin, 500 mg, one tablet twice a day for ten days.
- Ampicillin, 500 mg, two hours before meals and at bedtime for ten days.
- Prilosec, 20 mg once daily for three to four weeks.

Natural Therapies:

- Licorice (enhances the blood flow to the intestinal cells and heals the stomach mucus lining), one capsule three times a day with meals.
- Goldenseal (possesses a soothing effect to mucous membranes), one capsule three times a day with meals.
- Aloe vera juice (heals the mucous membranes), 2 oz. three times a day before meals.
- Gamma oryzanol (a compound found in rice-bran oil), 100 mg, three times a day for three to six weeks.

In his practice, Dr. Yutsis has found that 35 to 40 percent of his CFIDS patients harbor parasites, especially protozoa. After undergoing treatment, many of their symptoms were alleviated.

19.

MOVING UPWARD FROM THE DOWNHILL SYNDROME

When did the Downhill Syndrome become a recognized and treatable disease? Was it in 1974, when the tale of illness began for thirty-eight-year-old Albuquerque, New Mexico homemaker Nancy Kaiser—or when her continuing condition was revealed sixteen years later as a cover story in *Newsweek*?

Perhaps CFIDS took on official status when Dr. Jack Kevorkian assisted forty-two-year-old Judith Curren of Pembroke, Massachusetts to commit suicide on August 14, 1996. Mrs. Curren, a registered nurse suffering from CFIDS, took her own life in order to escape from the daily misery she had been experiencing for over a dozen years.

Whatever the case, patients have run the gamut from despair to hope.

TRUE VICTIMS

It's not so rare for victims of the Downhill Syndrome to seek peace in death. On March 29, 1996, Kathleen Kelly, age 47, called 911 and told the emergency service operator she was about to kill herself. Kathy asked the operator to explain to the Kelly family how much she loved them; then Kathy ended the phone call with a gunshot to her head.

Kathy Kelly is survived by her family, including her daughter, Holly, whose eighteenth birthday fell just three days before her mother's death. Kathy Kelly was reported to have said, "Tomorrow's Holly's birthday, and I can't even plan a party for her.

I did call and manage to order a cake." But all the time suicide was on Kathy's mind and a pistol was at hand to carry it out.

The CFIDS sufferer left a suicide note that began, "I died today from chronic fatigue. . . ." According to her sister, Maryan Wiedenfeld, Kathy's dying request was that people be made aware of this disease and the lack of treatment she received from her health maintenance organization (HMO). The HMO administrators and doctors refused to recognize that their health-care subscriber had a "real" disease. She paid her premiums and still, for over two years while Kathy suffered from the Downhill Syndrome, the HMO did nothing to relieve her agony. No doctors on its list of vendors dispensed any aid at all—this, despite the HMO knowing that Kathy didn't have the ability to get out of bed or to eat anything.

The woman's desire for death as a means of respite is laid out clearly enough, for Kathy had chronicled this last period in her life in a diary which she recorded by audiocassette. "Nothing really works anymore to help the pain," she said on March 23, 1996. "I get tired of saying things to other people about how I feel, so I decided not to anymore and I can just talk to you. I just want to be a normal person, and I can't."

It was a terribly frustrating set of daily circumstances that she faced, as much from not knowing the causes of her discomforts as from the discomforts themselves. For instance, on the audiotape she declares: "I'm going to die . . . I don't know what's the matter with me. But every day is worse and worse. I keep trying to be here, because I don't want to hurt anybody. . .

"Truthfully, I know I should be in a hospital. But nobody knows about this disease that I have . . . It's just too horrible . . . I'm not 'me' anymore. I wish I could just go and not hurt anybody . . . Sometimes I think I just might die in my sleep or something, because I'm very ill, and I don't really want to take my life. But I really can't take it too much longer, I know."

"God, I want to live! Don't you understand that?" Kathy cried into her audio diary. "Everybody thinks I want to die and that I am depressed, and I have to say this: Yes I am depressed, but I wasn't before I got ill. I was very happy . . . If I had a fatal illness, I think, forgive me, but I think I would be better off because somebody would know how it felt."

With the vague and indescribable symptoms of the Downhill Syndrome, she sensed that nobody understood, and this was the most frustrating part. In her suicide note, rather than an explanation, she offered more of a plea for understanding of CFIDS and asked for an attitude change by doctors. She wanted some kind of input from her HMO. This is what Kathy Kelly wrote:

"To doctors! I died today from chronic fatigue. Doctors don't understand the pain and weakness, some still believe it doesn't exist. I didn't die from prescription medicine or alcohol. I died because no one believed me in the medical profession . . . I can't live this way. It's been over two years and I'm getting worse. I can't go anywhere and don't have a moment free of pain . . . Somebody must bring this disease to the forefront and realize its devastation and whether it is contagious. I'd rather die than have my family or boyfriend get this horrific illness. It just affects everything."

"I can't even get an MRI out of my HMO . . . I'm not so much depressed as I am angry because the medical profession is too wrapped up in saving money rather than people."

"I love my family and don't want to hurt them, but I held on as long as I could . . . Good bye."

ANOTHER VICTIM

Donna Kay Sundberg, an inventory-control specialist with Rockwell International, had been selected the Rockwell "employee of the quarter" three months before she came down with the Downhill Syndrome. At age 41, this CFIDS victim died November 23, 1995, at home in Lawrenceville, Georgia, after she swallowed a lethal combination dose of the narcotics xanax and doxepin, washed down with alcohol.

Tom Sundberg, Donna's husband, remembered the last day of his wife's life. "She walked upstairs with a bowl of soup after I had helped her wash, bathe, and shave to try and get her ready to go to North Alabama for Thanksgiving. Our new grandbaby was supposed to come over the next morning.

"Next morning I got up, [our daughter] Crystal called and asked if Mom was up. I heard the TV playing, so I said, "Yes, I guess she's up." About fifteen minutes later I went upstairs and found her. They said she'd been dead for six to twelve hours."

Tom believes that his wife was the victim of an uncaring medical community that did not help her deal appropriately with her illness. "She'd been sick for six years, and had been dragging bottom the last year. Her doctors were not helpful," he said.

MOVING UPWARD FROM THE DOWNHILL SYNDROME

Six weeks after the 1990 *Newsweek* article came out, Jessica Valencia, age 44, arrived by ambulance at Dr. Yutsis' office. Living in a state of chronic fatigue was not part of her long-range plans. She intended to kill herself in a way that wasn't too messy—probably by carbon-monoxide poisoning in her garage with the door closed and the car motor running, she revealed much later.

Jessica lived in a small house in Rockville Centre, New York, and had worked as a dental hygienist until her Downhill Syndrome symptoms became so overwhelming that she couldn't even rise from her bed in the morning. Going to work became out of the question.

Jessica suffered from a variety of problems—all related to the complex of symptoms that have finally been identified as CFIDS. She had severe allergies to mold and mildew, generalized candidiasis with complicating yeast vaginitis, viral infections of multiple types, and an intestinal protozoan infection of *Entamoeba histolytica*, which produced frequent bouts of diarrhea interspersed with uncomfortable days of constipation.

Jessica was allergic to numerous foods, too, some of which she recognized and avoided, such as various grains, sardines, and cow's milk. By testing, Dr. Yutsis discovered other foods that caused her distress, including potatoes, tomatoes, string beans, cane sugar, apples, peaches, apricots, oranges, onions, black pepper, and chocolate. Certain fabrics like rayon, orlon, and dacron brought on sensitivity reactions for Jessica.

In addition, she suffered from just about every symptom of the Downhill Syndrome: fatigue, hives, headaches, belching from gastrointestinal gas, stomachache, periodic nausea, frequent vomiting, premenstrual syndrome, back pain, frequent sore throats, difficulty swallowing, hoarseness, depression, irritability, forgetfulness, poor concentration, total physical weakness, apathy, confusion, insomnia, sleeplessness, and swollen lymph glands.

All of these health problems comprised a kind of jigsaw puzzle for Dr. Yutsis to figure out. There was no single cause, but rather the complex that we now recognize as the Downhill Syndrome.

Dr. Yutsis broke down the symptoms into categories related to the body systems with which they were connected. Jessica became intrigued with correcting one symptom complex after another. Almost as an objective observer, she watched her body's reactions to various treatments and suggested alterations to Dr. Yutsis' procedures. He listened to his patient, and together they started her moving upward from the Downhill Syndrome.

It took two years of persistent therapy involving regular monthly visits to Dr. Yutsis and much self-help administration of nutrients, drugs, detoxification procedures, fasting, and various other health-promoting regimens. Finally, progress in Jessica's recovery became quite apparent, and eventually she reached complete normality.

One method of measuring her improvement over time was to note the circumstances involved with the transportation she used to travel to Dr. Yutsis's office. The ambulance that initially brought Jessica had long since been abandoned. In follow-up visits, her husband drove the patient in their family car. At first, she could only manage the long ride lying down on the back seat. After six months, Jessica still remained on the back seat but sat up. After another few months, she sat beside him in the front seat. Eventually, she drove herself accompanied by a companion. And finally, she drove alone.

Six years have passed since Jessica Valencia considered suicide as the solution to her Downhill Syndrome. Today, she is a normal mother and grandmother.

The Downhill Syndrome had been labeled by its victims "the twentieth-century plague." But now it's no longer "A Modern Medical Mystery" as it was designated in the *Newsweek* issue of November 12, 1990. As a result of investigations by clinicians like Dr. Pavel Yutsis, Dr. Majid Ali, Dr. Hermann Bueno, and others, CFIDS is being conquered.

As reported by Michelle Akers, a world-champion soccer player whose CFIDS attacks her regularly and often keeps her out of matches: "I know it's a real illness. I know it affects people to different degrees. I have been in bed. I have lost my life. I'm regaining some of it, but I will always be affected by this. I just think it's my responsibility to tell the world about it." And telling the world is what we have attempted to do in this book.

LOOKING AHEAD

The concept of the Downhill Syndrome has been created. Acknowledgment of it has widened physicians' horizons and provided patients with new diagnostic and treatment approaches. By determining and addressing the contributing factors, improvement in the patient's condition usually follows.

After reading this book, very few people will be doubtful about the multifactor nature of CFIDS. This very nature, however, brings us a mix of good and bad news. The good news is that we are no longer chasing "the magic bullet" for the CFIDS treatment, and are not pursuing the quest for the "golden key" that would open up a box labeled "CFIDS." The bad news is that because the factors are so varied, their challenge seems endless.

New findings are reported daily. According to Dr. Paul Cheney, about 40 percent of CFIDS patients demonstrate fingerprint abnormalities. Dr. Cheney has also studied energy metabolism in CFIDS patients by using bicycle ergometry. This test helps to determine the extent of oxygen utilization. Dr. Cheney determined that CFIDS patients' oxygen utilization was about 60 percent, compared to 100 percent in the healthy population.

Recently, interesting abnormalities have been found in the cerebellum (brain region) of CFIDS patients: research shows they have about an 81 percent reduction in cerebellar flow. Another hypothesis connects CFIDS to hormone deficiencies in the hypothalamus, pituitary, and adrenal glands.

Finally, Australian researchers, led by Drs. Hugh Dunstan and Neil McGregor, have found interesting abnormalities in the urine of CFIDS patients. According to Dr. Cheney, "these compounds, tagged CFS Urinary Marker 1 and 2 (CFSUM1 and CFSUM2), are thought to be genetically altered gut bacteria produced in response to pesticides in food. Although these compounds are not likely to be a cause of CFIDS, they may open new research avenues that will explain the disease." For readers of this book, these findings come as no surprise. The chapter on heavy metals and chemical toxicities presents these as important components of the Downhill Syndrome.

Looking ahead, we must admit our concern for the future of Downhill Syndrome patients. It is difficult to overestimate the amount of research needed to solve the Downhill Syndrome puzzle. Physicians and scientists, however, will continue their dedicated work, finding new understanding and treatment. These people will continue to spread the word about the debilitating nature of the disease. We owe that to the memories of Judith Curren, Kathleen Kelly, Donna Sundberg, and to the millions of Downhill Syndrome sufferers who are desperately seeking help.

REFERENCES

CHAPTER 1

Tracking Down a Mysterious Fatigue Epidemic

1. Boly, William. "Raggedy Ann town." *Hippocrates.* July/August 1987, pp. 31-40.

2. Garloch, Karen, "Medical sleuth closes in." *The Charlotte Observer,* September 4, 1990, pp. 1, 4.

3. Garloch, Karen. "Colleagues cautiously optimistic." *The Charlotte Observer,* September 4, 1990, pp. 1, 2.

4. Painter, Kim. "Chronic fatigue gains credibility." *USA Today,* September 18, 1990, Life, Section D, pp. 1D and 2D.

5. Patterson, David. "Association provides critical support for cutting-edge CFIDS research." *The CFIDS Chronicle,* Winter 1995.

CHAPTER 2

Signs and Symptoms of the Downhill Syndrome

1. Boly, William. "Raggedy Ann Town." *Hippocrates,* July/August 1987, pp. 31, 32.

2. Dawson, J. "Consensus on research into fatigue syndrome." *British Medical Journal,* 300:832, 1990.

3. Gantz, Nelson M. "An update on chronic fatigue syndrome." *Contemporary Internal Medicine,* April 1992, pp. 53-67.

4. *Ibid.*

5. Holmes, G.P.; Kaplan, J.E.; Gantz, N.M., et al. "Chronic fatigue syndrome: A working case definition." *Annals of Internal Medicine* 108:387, 1988.

6. Lloyd, A.R.; Wakefield, D.; Boughton, C., et al. "What is myalgic encephalomyelitis?" *Lancet,* 1:1286, 1988.

7. National Institute of Allergy and Infectious Diseases. *NIH Publications* Nos. 90-484, October 1990.

8. Sharpe, M.C.; Archard, L.C.; Banatvala, J.E., et al. "Chronic fatigue syndrome: Guidelines for research." *Journal of the Royal Society of Medicine,* 84:118, 1991.

CHAPTER 3

Searching for the Causes of The Downhill Syndrome

1. Archard, L.C.; Bowles, N.E.; Behan, P.O., et al. "Postviral fatigue syndrome: Persistence of enterovirus RNA in muscle and elevated creatine kinase." *Journal of the Royal Society of Medicine ,* 81:326, 1988.

2. Leary, Warren E. "Study shows viral mutation due to nutritional deficiency." *The New York Times,* May 1, 1995, p. A14.

3. *Ibid.*

4. Sheehan, Michael. "Was Pasteur wrong?" *Natural Health,* January/February 1992, pp. 41-44.

5. "The State of CFIDS Research, NIAID advisors release report. *The CFIDS Chronicles.* The Quarterly Publication of the Chronic Fatigue & Immune Dysfunction Syndrome Association of America, Summer 1996.

6. Yanick, Paul. "Chronic fatigue syndrome & immunosuppression." *Townsend Letter for Doctors,* April 1994, pp. 288-291.

7. Yousef, G.E.; Bell, E.J.; Maun, G.F., et al: "Chronic enterovirus infection in patients with postviral fatigue syndrome." *Lancet,* 1:146, 1988.

CHAPTER 4

Diagnosing The Downhill Syndrome

1. Ambrus, J.L., et al. "Interferon and interferon inhibitor levels in patients infected with VZV, AIDS, ARC, or Kaposi's sarcoma, and in normal individuals." *American Journal of Medicine* 87:405-407, 1989.

2. Caliguiri, M., et al. "Phenotypic and functional deficiency of natural killer cells in patients with chronic fatigue syndrome." *Journal of Immunology* 139:3306-3313, 1987.

3. Hofmann, B.O., et al. "Lymphocyte transformation response to pokeweed mitogen as a predictive marker for development of AIDS and AIDS related symptoms in homosexual men with HIV antibodies." *British Medical Journal* 295:293-297, 1987.

4. Mosca, J.D., et al. "Activation of HIV by herpesvirus infection: Identification of a region within the LTR that responds to a transacting factor encoded by herpes simplex virus I." *Proceedings of the National Academy of Sciences* 84:7408-7412, 1987.

5. DeFreitas, Elaine, et al. "Retroviral sequences related to human T-lymphotropic virus type II in patients with chronic fatigue immune dysfunction syndrome." *Proceedings of the National Academy of Sciences* 88:2922-2926, 1991.

6. Dinarello, C.A., and J. W. Mier. "Lymphokines." *New England Journal of Medicine* 371:940-945, 1987.

7. Fujimoto, J., et al. *Journal of Experimental Medicine* 159:752-766, 1983.

8. Garman, R.D., et al. "B-cell stimulatory factor functions as a second signal for IL-2 production by mature murine T-cells." *Proceedings of the National Academy of Scineces* 84:7629-7633, 1987.

9. Gordon, J., et al. "CD-23 a multifunctional receptor/lymphokine?" *Immunology Today* 10:153-157, 1989.

10. Greenberg, S.B. "Human interferon in viral diseases." *Antiviral Chemotherapy* 891:383-423, 1987.

11. Jefferis, R., and D.S. Kumaranatne. "Selective IgG subclass deficiency: quantification and clinical relevance." *Clinical and Experimental Immunology* 81:357-367, 1990.

12. O'Garra, A. "Interleukins and the immune system." *Lancet* 1:943-944, 1989.

13. Sethi, K.K., and H. Naher. "Elevated titers of cell-free interleukin-2 receptor in serum and CSF of patients with AIDS. *Immunology Letter* 13:179-184, 1986.

14. Wolf, R.E., and W.G. Brelsford. "Soluble interleukin-2 receptors in SLE." *Arthritis and Rheumatism* 31:729-735, 1988.

CHAPTER 5

Metabolic Immunodepression

1. Bronsgeest-Schoute, H.C.; van Gent, C.M.; Luten, J.B., et al. "The effect of various intakes of omega-3 fatty acids on the blood lipid composition in healthy human subjects." *American Journal of Clinical Nutrition* 34:1752-1757, 1981.

2. Fehily, A.M.; Burr, M.L.; Phillips, K.M., et al. "The effect of fatty fish on plasma lipid and lipoprotein concentrations." *American Journal of Clinical Nutrition* 38:349-351, 1983.

3. Gerich, J.E.; Charles, M.A.; Levin, S.R.; Forsham, P.H.; Grodsky, G.M. "In vitro inhibition of pancreatic glucagon secretion by diphenylhydantoin." *Journal of Clinical Endocrinology* 35:823-824, 1972.

4. Illingworth, D.R.; Harris, W.S.; Connor, W.E. "Inhibition of low density lipoprotein synthesis by dietary omega-3 fatty acids in humans." *Arteriosclerosis* 4:270-275, 1984.

5. Maguire, J.H.; Murthy, A.R.; Hall, I.H. "Hypolipidemic activity of antiepileptic 5-phenylhydantoins in mice." *European Journal of Pharmacology* 117:135-138, 1985.

6. Nikkila, E.A.; Kaste, M.; Ehnholm, C.; Viikari, J. "Elevation of high-density lipoprotein in epileptic patients treated with phenytoin." *Journal of Scandinavian Medicine* 204:517-520, 1978.

7. Phillipson, B.E.; Rothrock, D.W.; Connor, W.E., et al. "Reduction of plasma lipids, lipoproteins, and apoproteins by dietary fish oils in patients with hypertriglyceridemia." *New England Journal of Medicine* 312:1210-1216, 1985.

8. Yanick, Paul. "Chronic fatigue syndrome & immunosuppression." *Townsend Letter for Doctors*, April 1994, pp. 288-291.

INTRODUCTION TO PART II

Henig, Robin Marantz. *A Dancing Matrix: Voyages Along the Viral Frontier.* (New York: Alfred A. Knopf, 1993), pp. 58-61.

CHAPTER 6

Chronic Epstein-Barr Virus

1. Andiman, W.A. "The Epstein-Barr virus infections in childhood." *Journal of Pediatrics* 95:171, 1979.

2. Buchwald, D.; Sullivan, J.L.; Komarolf, A.L. "Frequency of chronic active Epstein-Barr virus infection in a general medical practice." *Journal of the American Medical Association* 257:2302, 1987.

3. Donovan, Patrick M. "Chronic mononucleosis-like syndrome: Primary EBV infection or indicator of immune system dysfunction?" In Pizzorno & Murray, *Chronic Mononucleosis,* November 16, 1987, pp. 1-4.

4. Dubois, R.E.; Seely, J.R.; Brus, I.; et al. "Chronic mononucleosis syndrome." *Southern Medical Journal* 77:1376-1382, 1984.

5. Henle, W.; Henle, G.; Lennette, E.T. "The Epstein-Barr virus." *Scientific American* 241:229, 1973.

6. Holms, Gary P.; Kaplan, Jonathan E.; Gantz, Nelson M; et al. "Chronic fatigue syndrome: A working case definition." *Annals of Internal Medicine* 108:387-389, 1988.

7. Jaret, Peter. "Chronic fatigue syndrome: An update." *Glamour,* November 1992.

8. Jones, J.F.; Ray, G.; Minnich, L.L.; et al. "Evidence for active Epstein-Barr virus infection in patients with persistent unexplained illness: Elevated anti-early antigen antibodies." *Annals of Internal Medicine* 102:1-7, 1985.

9. Jones, J.F. "Chronic Epstein-Barr virus infection in children." *Pediatric Infectious Diseases* 5:503-504, 1986.

10. Miller, G.; Niederman, J.D.; Andrews, L. "Prolonged oropharyngeal excreation of Epstein-Barr virus after infectious mononucleosis." *New England Journal of Medicine* 288:132, 1977.

11. Pawlyna, Andrea. "The baby boomer disease." *The Sun,* Today Section D, July 16, 1987, pp. 1D, 3D.

12. Petersdorf, R.G.; Adams, R.D.; Braunwald, E.; et al. *Harrison's Principles of Internal Medicine* 10th ed. (New York: McGraw-Hill, 1983).

13. Rapp, C.E., and J.F. Hewetson. "Infectious mononucleosis and the Epstein-Barr virus." *American Journal of Diseases in Children* 132:78, 1978.

14. Rocchi, G.; DeFelici, A.; Ragona, G.; et al. "Quantitative evaluation of Epstein-Barr virus-infected mononuclear peripheral blood leukocytes in infectious mononucleosis." *New England Journal of Medicine* 296:132, 1977.

15. Straus, S.E.; Tosato, F.; Armstrong, G.; et al. "Persisting illness and fatigue in adults with evidence of Epstein-Barr virus infection." *Annals of Internal Medicine* 102:7-16, 1985.

16. Tobi, M.; Morag, A.; Ravid, Z.; et al. "Prolonged atypical illness associated with serological evidence of persistent Epstein-Barr virus infection." *Lancet* I:61-64, 1982.

CHAPTER 7

The Cytomegalovirus (CMV)

1. Goodgame, R.W. "Gastrointestinal cytomegalovirus disease." *Annals of Internal Medicine* 119:924, 1993.

2. Henig, Robin Marantz. *A Dancing Matrix: Voyages Along the Viral Frontier.* (New York: Alfred A. Knopf, 1993), p. 30.

3. *Ibid*, p. 30.

CHAPTER 8

The Human Herpesvirus-VI (HHV-6)

1. Agut, H.; Huraux, J.M.; Colandre, H.; Montagnier, L. "Susceptibility of human herpesvirus 6 to acyclovir and ganciclovir." *Lancet* 2:626, 1989.

2. Alexander, E.L.; Kumar, A.J.; Kozachuk, W.E. Letters: "The chronic fatigue syndrome controversy." *Annals of Internal Medicine* 117(4):343-344, August 15, 1992.

3. Altman, Lawrence K. "Experts unable to link chronic fatigue to virus." *The New York Times*, September 24, 1991, p. C5.

4. Asano, Y.; Nakashima, T.; Yoshikawa, T.; Suga, S.; Yazaki, T. "Severity of human herpesvirus-6 viremia and clinical findings in infants with exanthem subitum." *Journal of Pediatrics* 118:891-895, 1991.

5. Asano, Y.; Suga, S.; Yoshikawa, T.; Urisu, A.; Yazaki, T. "Human herpesvirus type 6 infection (exanthem subitum) without fever." *Journal of Pediatrics* 115:264-265, 1989.

6. Asano, Y.; Yoshikawa, T.; Suga, S.; Yazaki, T.; Kondo, K.; Yamanishi, K. "Fatal fulminant hepatitis in an infant with human herpesvirus-6 infection." *Lancet* 335:862-863, 1990.

7. Aubin, J-T.; Collandre, H.; Candotti, D., et al. "Several groups among human herpesvirus 6 strains can be distinguished by Southern Blotting and polymerase chain reaction." *Journal of Clinical Microbiology* 29:367-372, 1991.

8. Buchwald, D.; Cheney, P.R.; Peterson, D.L.; Berch, H.; Wormsley, S.B.; Geiger, A.; Ablashi, D.V.; Salahuddin, S.Z.; Saxinger, C.; Biddle, R.; Kikinis,R.; Jolesz, F.A.; Folds, T.; Balachandran, N.; Peter, J.B.; Gallo, R.C.; and Komarofff, A.L. "A chronic illness characterized by fatigue, neurologic and immunologic disorders, and active human herpesvirus type 6 infection." *Annals of Internal Medicine* 116:103-113, 1992.

9. Dubedat, S. and Kappagoda, N. "Hepatitis due to human herpesvirus-6." *Lancet* 2:1463-1464, 1989.

10. Efstathiou, S.; Gompels, U.A.; Craxton, M.A., et al. "DNA homology between a novel human herpes virus (HHV-6) and human cytomegalovirus." *Lancet* 1:63-64, 1988.

11. Fox, J.D.; Briggs, M.; Ward, P.A., et al. "Human herpesvirus 6 in salivary glands." *Lancet* 336:590-594, 1990.

12. Fox, J.D.; Ward, P.; Briggs, M.; Irving, W.; Stammers, T.G.; Tedder, R.S. "Production of IgM antibody to HHV-6 in reactivation and primary infection." *Journal of Epidemiology and Infectious Diseases* 104:289-296, 1990.

13. Harnett, G.E.; Farr, T.J.; Pietroboni, G.R., et al. "Frequent shedding of HHV-6 in saliva." *Journal of Medicine and Virology* 30:128-130, 1990.

14. Irving, W.I.; Ratnamohan, M.; Hueston, L.C.; Chapman, J.R.; Cunningham, A.L. "Dual antibody rises to cytomegalovirus and human herpesvirus type 6: frequency of occurrence in CMV infections and evidence for genuine ractivity to both viruses." *Journal of Infectious Diseases* 161:910-916, 1990.

15. Knowles, W.A. and Gardner, S.D. "High prevalence of antibody to human herpesvirus-6 and seroconversion associated with rash in two infants." *Lancet* 2:912-913, 1988.

16. Komaroff, A.L.; Berch, H.; Ablashi, D.V. Letters: "The chronic fatigue syndrome controversy." *Annals of Internal Medicine* 117(4):343-344, August 15, 1992.

17. Kondo, K.; Hayakawa, Y.; Mori, H., et al. "Detection by polymerase chain reaction amplification of human herpesvirus 6 DNA in peripheral blood of patients with exanthem subitum." *Journal of Clinical Microbiology* 28:970-974, 1990.

18. Lawrence, G.L; Chee, M.; Craxton, M.A.; Gompels, U.A.; Honess, R.W.; Barrell, B.G. "Human herpesvirus 6 is closely related to human cytomegalovirus." *Journal of Virology* 64:287-299, 1990.

19. Linnavuori, K.; Peltola, H.; Hovi, T. "Serology versus clinical signs or symptoms and main laboratory findings in the diagnosis of exanthema subitum (roseola infantum)." *Pediatrics* 89:103-106, 1992.

20. Niederman, J.C.; Kaplan, M.H.; Liu, F.R.; Brown, N.A. "Clinical and serological features of human herpesvirus-6 infection in three adults." *Lancet* 2:817-819, 1988.

21. Pruksananonda, P.; Hall, C.B.; Insel, R.A.; Pellett, P.E.; Stewart, J.A. "Acute human herpesvirus 6 (HHV-6) infection in normal American children [Abstract 1]. *Program and Abstracts of the Thirtieth Interscience Conference on Antimicrobial Agents and Chemotherapy.* (Washington, D.C.: American Society for Microbiology, 1990).

22. Salahuddin, S.Z.; Ablashi, DV.; Markham, P.D., et al. "Isolation of a new virus, HBLV, in patients with lymphoproliferative disorders." *Science* 234:596-601, 1986.

23. Sobue, R.; Miyazaki, H.; Okamoto, M., et al. "Fulminant hepatitis in primary human herpesvirus-6 infection." *New England Journal of Medicine* 324:1290, 1991.

24. Steeper, T.A.; Horwitz, C.A.; Ablashi, D.V., et al. "The spectrum of clinical and laboratory findings resulting from human herpesvirus-6 (HHV-6) in patients with mononucleosis-like illnesses not resulting from Epstein-Barr virus or cytomegalovirus." *American Journal of Clinical Pathology* 93:776-783, 1990.

25. Suga, S.; Yoshikawa, T.; Asano, Y.; Yazaki, T.; Hirata, S. "Human herpesvirus-6 infection (exanthem subitum) without rash." *Pediatrics* 83:1003-1006, 1989.

26. Tajiri, H.; Nose, O.; Baba, K.; Okada, S. "Human herpesvirus-6 infection with liver injury in neonatal hepatitis." *Lancet* 335:863, 1990.

27. Takahashi, K.; Sonoda, S.; Kawakami, K., et al. "Human herpesvirus 6 and exanthem subitum." *Lancet* 1:1463, 1988.

28. Tedder, R.; Briggs, M.; Cameron, C.H.; Honess, R.; Robertson, D.; Whittle, H. "A novel lymphotropic herpesvirus." *Lancet* 2:390-392, 1987.

29. Ueda, K.; Kusuhara, K.; Hirose, M., et al. "Exanthem subitum and antibody to human herpesvirus-6." *Journal of Infectious Diseases* 159:750-752, 1989.

30. Ward, K.N.; Gray, J.J.; Efstathiou, S. "Brief report: primary human herpesvirus 6 infection in a patient following liver transplantation from a seropositive donor." *Journal of Medicine and Virology* 28:69-72, 1989.

31. Yamanishi, K.; Shiraki, K.; Kondo, T, et al. "Identification of human herpesvirus-6 as a causal agent for exanthem subi-

tum." *Lancet* 1:1065-1067, 1988.

32. Yoshiyama, H.; Suzuki, E.; Yoshida, T.; Kajii, T.; Yamamoto, N. "Role of human herpesvirus 6 infection in infants with exanthem subitum." *Pediatric Infectious Diseases Journal* 9:71-74, 1990.

CHAPTER 9

Human Retroviruses As Disease Factors

1. Bohannon, R.C.; Donehower, L.A.; Ford, R.J. "Isolation of a type D retrovirus from B-cell lymphomas of a patient with AIDS." *Journal of Virology* 65:5663-5672, 1991.

2. Cowley, Geoffrey and Mary Hager. "A clue to chronic fatigue." *Newsweek*, Lifestyle-Medicine Section, 1991.

3. DeFreitas, Elaine; Hilliard, Brendan; Cheney, Paul R.; et al. "Retroviral sequences related to human T-lymphotropic virus type II in patients with chronic fatigue immune dysfunction syndrome." *Proceedings of the National Academy of Sciences USA* 88:2922:2926, April 1991.

4. Gallo, Robert. *Virus Hunting: AIDS, Cancer, and the Human Retrovirus: A Story of Scientific Discovery.* (New York City: Basic Books, 1991), p. 96.

5. Garry, R.F.; Fermin, C.D.; Hart, D.J.; et al. "Detection of a human intracisternal A-type retroviral particle antigenically related to HIV." *Science* 250:1127-1129, 1990.

6. Hall, W.W.; Liu, C.R.; Schneewind, O.; et al. "Deleted HTLV-1 provirus in blood and cutaneous lesions of patients with mycosis fungoides." *Science* 253:317-320, 1991.

7. Heneine, Walid; Woods, Toni C.; Sinha, Saswati D.; et al. "Lack of evidence for infection with known human and animal retroviruses in patients with chronic fatigue syndrome." *Clinical Infectious Diseases* 18(Suppl. 1): S121-125, 1994.

8. Heneine, Walid; Woods, Toni; Khan, Ali S.; et al. "Investigation of retroviral involvement in chronic fatigue syndrome." *Proceedings of the International CFS/ME Research Conference,* Albany, New York, October 3-4, 1992.

9. Henig, Robin Marantz. *A Dancing Matrix: Voyages Along the Viral Frontier.* (New York City: Alfred A. Knopf, 1993), pp. 58-61.

10. Khabbaz, R.F.; Heneine, W.; George, J.R., et al. "First isolation of a simian immunodeficiency virus from a human." *Program and Abstracts: IX International Conference on AIDS (Berlin)*, 1993.

11. Lagaye, S.; Vexiau, P.; Morzov, V.; et al. "Human spumaretro-virus-related sequences in the DNA of leukocytes from patients with Graves disease." *Proceedings of the National Academy of Sciences USA* 89:10070-10074, 1992.

12. Levine, Arnold J. *Viruses.* (New York City: Scientific American Library, 1992), p. 38.

13. Winslow, Ron. "Virus may have role in causing chronic fatigue." *The Wall Street Journal*, September 16, 1991.

14. Winslow, Ron. "Chronic fatigue link to virus gains support." *The Wall Street Journal*, September 23, 1991.

CHAPTER 10

Potential Cures for Viral Infections

1. Badgley, Laurence. *Healing AIDS Naturally.* (San Bruno, CA: Human Energy Press, 1986), p. 63.

2. Bauer, R. and H. Wagner. In Wagner, H. and Farnsworth, N.R. (eds.) *Economic and Medicinal Plant Research*, Vol. 5. (London: Academic Press, 1991).

3. Benjamini, Eli and Sidney Leskowitz. *Immunology, A Short Course*, Second Ed. (New York City: Wiley-Liss, 1991), p. 400.

4. Bone, Kerry. "New research on HIV-1: Implications for phy-totherapy." (Letters to the Editor) *Townsend Letter for Doctors*, July 1995, pp. 80-82.

5. Donovan, Patrick M. "Chronic mononucleosis-like syndrome: Primary EBV infection or indicator of immune system dys-function?" In *Chronic Mononucleosis*, Joseph E. Pizzorno and Michael T. Murray (Eds.), (Seattle, WA: Bastyr University, November 16, 1987).

6. Drake, Donald C. "Chronic fatigue syndrome, AIDS-type virus linked." *The Philadelphia Inquirer,* September 4, 1990, Section A, p. 1.

7. Fettner, Ann Giudici. *Viruses, Agents of Change* (New York City: McGraw-Hill Publishing, Co., 1990), p. 236.

8. Stites, Daniel P. and Abba I. Terr. *Basic and Clinical Immunology,* Seventh Ed., (Norwalk, Connecticut: Appleton & Lange, 1991), pp. 92-96.

9. Walker, Morton. "Carnivora therapy for cancer and AIDS." *Explore* 3(5):10-15, November/December 1992.

10. Walker, Morton. "The Carnivora cure for cancer, AIDS, & Other Pathologies." *Townsend Letter for Doctors,* June 1991, pp. 412-416.

11. Walker, Morton. "The Carnivora cure for cancer, AIDS & Other Pathologies—Part II." *Townsend Letter for Doctors,* May 1992, pp. 329-359.

12. Walker, Morton. "Venus' Flytrap—cancer and AIDS, fighter of the future?" *Natural Health,* September/October 1992, pp. 44, 45.

CHAPTER 11

The Factor of Yeast in CFIDS

1. Crook, W.B. *Chronic Fatigue Syndrome & The Yeast Connection.* (Professional Books, 1992).

2. Jessup, C. Synopsis of comments regarding her work with 1,100 patients from 1980 to 1989. Medical support for the Candida/Human Interaction. A Compendium, edited by William G. Crook, M.D., pp. 217-218.

3. Kroker, G.F. "Food Allergy and Intolerance," by Jonathan Brostoff and Stephen J. Challacombe (Balliere Tindall/W.B. Saunders, 1987), pp. 850-870.

4. Landay, A.L., Jessop, C., Lennette, E.T., et al. "Chronic Fatigue Syndrome: Clinical Condition Associated with Immune Activation." *Lancet,* 338:707-712, 1991.

5. Staver, S. "Meeting Sheds Light on Chronic Fatigue." *American Medical News,* May 26, 1989.

6. Truss, O.C. *"The Missing Diagnosis."* The Missing Diagnosis, Inc., 1983.

7. Yutsis, Pavel I. "Candida Albicans: A Fresh Look at the Existing Controversy." *Explore Magazine,* Volume 7, No. 2, 1996, pp. 18-20.

CHAPTER 12

Dental Amalgam Toxicity

1. Casdorph, H.R. and M. Walker. *Toxic Metal Syndrome: How Metal Poisoning Affects Your Brain.* (Garden City Park, New York: Avery Publishing, 1995).

2. "Cremation pollution." *The New York Times,* August 21, 1990.

3. Drasch, G., et al. "Mercury burden of human fetal and infant tissues." *European Journal of Pediatrics* 153:607-610, 1994.

4. Faber, W.J., and Walter, M. *Pain, Pain Go Away.* (San Jose, California: Ishi Press International, 1990).

5. Faber, W.J., and Walker, M. *Instant Pain Relief.* (Milwaukee, Wisconsin: Biological Publications, 1991).

6. Hahn, L.J.; Kloiber, R.; Vimy, M.J.; et al. "Dental 'silver' tooth fillings: a source of mercury exposure revealed by whole-body image scan and tissue analysis." *The FASEB Journal* 3:2641, 1989.

7. Huggins, H.A. "Autoimmune & carcinogenic responses to dental materials: diagnosis & treatment." *Explore More* 6(3):64-65.

8. Huggins, H.A. *It's All in Your Head: The Link Between Mercury Amalgams and Illness* (Garden City Park, New York: Avery Publishing Group, 1993), pp. 78-79.

9. Royal, F.F. "Are dentists contributing to our declining health?" *Townsend Letter for Doctors,* May 1990, pp. 311-314.

10. Queen, H.L. *Chronic Mercury Toxicity: New Hope Against an Endemic Disease.* (Colorado Springs, Colorado: Queen & Co. Health Communications, Inc., 1988).

11. Sehnert, K.W.; Jacobson, G.; Sullivan, K. "Is mercury toxicity an autoimmune disorder?" *Townsend Letter for Doctors & Patients,* Oct. 1995, pp. 134-137.

12. Sehnert, K.W. "Autoimmune disorders," *Advance,* January 1995, pp. 47, 48.

13. Walker, M. *The Chelation Way: The Complete Book of Chelation Therapy.* (Garden City Park, New York: Avery Publishing, 1990).

14. Warren, T. *Beating Alzheimer's: A Step Towards Unlocking the Mysteries of Brain Diseases.* (Garden City Park, New York: Avery Publishing Group, 1991), p. 171.

15. Ziff, S. "Dental offices polluting the water supply with mercury?" *Dental & Dental Facts* 2(6):2, 1989.

CHAPTERS 13 AND 14

How Heavy Metals and Chemicals Poison The Body;

How To Eliminate Heavy Metals and Chemical Pollutants From Your Body

1. Brody, J. "DDT linked to pancreatic cancer in humans." *The New York Times,* Section C, June 17, 1992.

2. Chartoff, M.D. "Study says children at risk from pesticides." *Safe Food News,* Fall 1993, p. 1.

3. EPA news release, November 4, 1977.

4. HEW news release, June 9, 1978.

5. Hodge, R. "Washington bulletin: detoxing your lawn." *Longevity,* March 1992, p. 26.

6. National Academy of Sciences news report, August 1978, p. 4.

7. "Pesticides in produce may threaten kids." *Science News* 144:1, July 3, 1993, p. 1.

8. *Ibid.,* p. 11.

9. Raldolph, T.G. *An Alternative Approach to Allergies.* (New York: Harper & Row, Publishers, 1989), pp. 237-247.

10. Rapp, D.J. with Bamberg, D. *The Impossible Child: A Guide For Caring Teachers and Parents in School, at Home.* (Buffalo, NY: Practical Allergy Research Foundation, 1986), p. 3.

11. "Report on carcinogenesis bioassay of dieldrin." HEW

Technical Report Series, no. 22, Washington, D.C., 1978.

12. "Report on carcinogenesis bioassay of technical grade chlordecone (Kepone)," HEW, Technical Background Information Series, Bethesda, MD, January 1976.

13. Rogers, Sherry A. *Tired or Toxic? A Blueprint for Health.* (Prestige Publishing, 1989), pp. 16-20.

14. Smith, B.L. "Organic foods vs. supermarket foods: Element levels." *Journal of Applied Nutrition* 45(1):35-39, 1993.

15. Winter, R. *Cancer-Causing Agents: A Preventive Guide.* (New York: Crown Publishers, Inc., 1979).

CHAPTER 15

Disease Symptoms From Allergies

1. Black, D.W.; Rathe, A.; Goldstein, R.B. "Environmental illness: a controlled study of 26 subjects with '20th century disease.'" *JAMA* 264(24):31663169, December 26, 1990.

2. Dickey, L.D. *Clinical Ecology.* (Springfield, IL: Charles C. Thomas, 1976).

3. Jones, M.M. "Leaky Gut: A Common Problem With Food Allergies." *Mastering Food Allergies* VIII (5):2, September/October 1993.

4. Mackarness, R. *Eating Dangerously: The Hazards of Hidden Allergies.* (New York: Harcourt Brace Jovanovich, 1976), pp. 125-128.

5. Mandell, M. and Scanlon, L.W. *Dr. Mandell's 5-Day Allergy Relief System.* (New York: Thomas Y. Crowell, 1979).

6. Mandell, M. "Food allergy, food addiction, obesity, alcoholism and chemical susceptibility. The clinical significance of reactions to ethyl alcohols derived from foods and petroleum." *Journal of the International Academy of Metabology.* II(I):72-87, March, 1973.

7. Randolph, T.G. and Moss, R.W. *An Alternative Approach to Allergies.* (New York: Lippincott & Crowell, 1980).

8. Randolph, T.G. *Environmental Medicine—Beginnings & Bibliographies of Clinical Ecology.* (Fort Collins, CO: Clinical Ecology Publications, Inc., 1987).

9. Rinkel, H.J. "The management of clinical allergy, I. General considerations." *Archives of Otolaryngology* (Chicago) 76:491, 1962.

10. Rinkel, H.J. "The management of clinical allergy, II. Etiologic factors and skin titration." *Archives of Otolaryngology* (Chicago) 77:42, 1963.

11. Rinkel, H.J. "The management of clinical allergy, III. Inhalant allergy therapy." *Archives of Otolaryngology* (Chicago) 77:205, 1963.

12. Rinkel, H.J. "The management of clinical allergy, IV. Food and mold allergy." *Archives of Otolaryngology* (Chicago) 77:302, 1963.

CHAPTER 16

Tests and Treatments For Allergies

1. Jones, M.H. "Leaky gut: a common problem with food allergies." *Mastering Food Allergies* VIII(5):2, Sept/Oct 1993.

2. Miller, J.B. *Relief at Last! Neutralization for Food Allergy and Other Illnesses.* (Springfield, IL: Charles C. Thomas, 1987).

3. *Ibid.* p. 12.

4. Walker, B.M. "Olympian battles CFIDS—soccer star integrates CFIDS into game of life." *The CFIDS Chronicle,* Vol.9 No. 3 Summer 1996, pp. 27-29.

5. Wunderlich, R.C. *Fatigue Revisited.* (St. Petersburg, FL: Wunderlich, 1992), p. 19

CHAPTER 17

Underactive Thyroid—Another Contributing Factor

1. Balch, J.F. and Balch, P.A. *Prescription for Nutritional Healing*

(Garden City Park, NY: Avery Publishing Group, 1990), p. 213.

2. Barnes, B. and Galton, L. *Hypothyroidism: the Unsuspected Illness* (New York: Harper and Row, Publishers, 1976).

3. Brody, J.E. "Underactive thyroids are treatable but often missed." *The New York Times*, March 29, 1995, p. C10.

4. Galton, L. "Low thyroid—is it sapping your energy?" *Family Circle Magazine*, October, 1973.

5. Hendler, S.S. *The Doctors' Vitamin and Mineral Encyclopedia* (New York: Fireside, 1991), pp. 147, 148.

6. Mindell, E. *Earl Mindell's New and Revised Vitamin Bible* (New York: Warner Books, 1985), pp. 89-91.

7. Peat, R. "Thyroid: misconceptions." Ray Peat's Newsletter, *Townsend Letter for Doctors*, November, 1993.

8. Smolle, J.; Wawschin, O.; Hayn, H., et al. "Serum levels of vitamin A and carotene in thyroid-disease." *Journal of Australian Medicine* 10:71-73, 1983.

9. Op. cit., Berkow and Fletcher, p. 1083.

10. Tintera, J.W. *Hypoadrenaocorticism*, 9th printing. (Adrenal Metabolic Research Society of the Hypoglycemia Foundation, Inc., 1980).

11. *Ibid.* p. 22.

12. Wilson, E.D. *Wilson's Syndrome, Doctor's Manual* (Longwood, Florida: Muskeegee Medical Publishing Co., 1991), p. 1.

13. Wilson, E.D. *Wilson's Syndrome, The Miracle of Feeling Well* (Orlando, Florida: Cornerstone Publishing Co., 1991).

14. *Ibid.* pp. 184-203.

CHAPTER 18

Parasites As Disease Factors

1. Brown, J.P. "Role of gut bacterial flora in nutrition and health: A review of recent advances in bacteriological techniques, metabolism, and factors affecting flora composition." *CRC*

reviews in *Food Science and Nutrition* 8:229-336, 1977.

2. Freudenheim, M. "Drug companies discount ulcer treatment advice." *The New York Times*, February 10, 1994, p. 1.

3. Goodwin, A. "Enzyme-linked immunosorbent assay for H. pylori: correlation with presence of H pylorids in gastric mucosa." *Journal of Infectious Diseases* 82:245, 1987.

4. Goodwin, A. "Helicobacter gastritis and peptic ulceration." *Journal of Clinical Pathology* 39:353, 1986.

5. Haenel, H. and Bendig, J. "Intestinal flora in health and disease." *Progress in Food and Nutrition Science* 1:21-64, 1975.

6. Jones, W. et al. "Helicobacter-like organisms on the gastric mucosa: culture, histological and serological studies." *Journal of Clinical Pathology* 37:1002, 1984.

7. Lior, F. et al. "Catalase, peroxidase, and SOD activities in Helicobacter species." In Pearson, B. (ed). Helicobacter III. Proceedings of the Third Intl. Workshop on *Helicobacter infections.* (London: PHLS, 1985), p. 226.

8. Marshall, B. et al. "Unidentified curved bacilli in the stomach of patients with gastritis and peptic ulceration." *Lancet* i:1311, 1984.

9. Marshall, B. et al. "Unidentified curved bacilus on gastric epithelium in active chronic gastritis." *Lancet* i:1273, 1983.

10. Marshall, B. et al. "Prospective double-blind trial of duodenal ulcer relapse after eradication of Helicobacter pylori." *Lancet* 24:1437, Dec. 1988.

11. Marshall, B. et al. "Attempt to fulfill Koch's postulates for Helicobacter pylori." *Medical Journal of Australia* 42:436, 1985.

12. Marshall, B. "Barry Marshall, M.D.: *Helicobacter pylori.*" *Dysbiosis: a clinical symposium* (New York City: Great Smokies Diagnostic Laboratory, May 2,1992), pp. 3-5. 1992), pp. 3-5. 1992), pp. 3-5. 1992), pp. 3-5. 1992), pp. 3-5.

13. Mielants, H. et al. "Intestinal mucosal permeability in inflammatory rheumatic diseases. II. Role of disease." *Journal of Rheumatology* 18(3):394-400, 1991.

14. *Op. cit.* Gittleman, p. 45.

15. *Ibid.* p. 53.

16. Moore, W.E.C. and Holdeman, L.V. *Cancer Research* 35:3418-3420, 1975.

17. Neva, F.A. "Parasitic diseases of the GI tract in the United States." *DM*, June 3, 1972.

18. Savage, D.C. *Microbial Pathogenicity in Man and Animals*, H. Smith and J.H. Pearce, (eds), 1972, pp. 25-57.

19. Warren, R. "Unidentified curved bacilus on gastric epithelium in active chronic gastritis (letter)." *Lancet* I:1273, 1983.

CHAPTER 19

Moving Upward From The Downhill Syndrome

1. Becker, Sandy E., Midwest CFIDS Conference, *The CFIDS Chronicle*, Vol. 9 No. 3 Summer 1996, pp. 62-65.

2. Cowley, G.; Hager, M.; Joseph, N. "Chronic fatigue syndrome: a modern medical mystery." *Newsweek.* November 12, 1990, pp. 62-70.

3. Schmidt, P. "In memory of Donna Sundberg & Kathleen Kelly." *The CFIDS Chronicle*, Vol. 9 No. 3 Summer 1996, p.25.

4. Taubman, B. "Dr. Death has second thoughts on suicide No. 35." *New York Post*, August 18, 1996, p.12.

5. Walker, B.M. "Olympian battles CFIDS—soccer star integrates CFIDS into game of life." *The CFIDS Chronicle*, Vol. 9 No. 3 Summer 1996, pp. 27-29.

6. Wrenn, F.T. "In memory of Donna Sundberg & Kathleen Kelly." *The CFIDS Chronicle*, Vol. 9 No. 3 Summer 1996, pp. 26.

INDEX

A

ABAVCA, as treatment for viral infections, 74
Acute acquired Cytomegalovirus infection, 55
AIDS, 5, 6, 26, 28
    effect of protozoa on, 150-152
    See also HIV.
Akers, Michelle, 161-162
Ali, Majid, M.D., 114-115, 161
Allergens. *See* Antigens.
Allergies
    chemical, CFIDS and, 119-120
    chemical, cytotoxic tests for, 127
    chemical, types of, 153
    definition of, 111-112
    food, cytotoxic tests for, 127
    food, fasting to determine, 125-126
    food, origins of, 116
    food, symptoms produced by, 116-118
    nutritional formulas to relieve, 128-133
    origins of, 114-115
    preservatives, food, 118-119
    symptoms of, in CFIDS patients, 112-113
    techniques to diagnose and treat, 122-128
    treatment, effect of, on CFIDS patients, 133
    See also Chemicals; Environmental illness; Heavy metals.
Alpha-Interferon, 29. *See also* Interferon.
Alpha-Interferon Serum Level, 29

Aluminum, 98-99

Amalgam, dental
    candidiasis and, 94
    CFIDS and, 88
    removal of, 92-94
    substitutes for, 93
    See also Mercury; Mercury
        poisoning.

Amino acids, as treatment for
    viral infections, 74

Antigens, 112, 114

Arsenic, 97

Askanazi, Jeffrey, M.D., 38-39

B

B cells, 27-29. *See also*
    Lymphocytes.

Bacteria, 145, 146. *See also*
    Helicobacter pylori;
    Parasites.

Badgley, Laurence, M.D., 72

Baker, Gloria, 10

Beck, Melinda, Ph.D., 21-22

Bell, David, M.D., 5-7, 68, 69,
    111

Bioflavonoids, 108

Blastocystis hominis, 146-147,
    152. *See also* Protozoa.

Bueno, Dr. Hermann, 151, 152,
    161

C

Cadmium, 97-98

Candida albicans, as promoter
    of disease, 80. *See also*
    Candidiasis.

Candidiasis
    dental amalgam and, 94
    diagnosis of, 80-83
    potential damage of, 79-80
    treatments for, 83-85

Canditoxins, 79

Carnivora®, as treatment for
    viral infections, 74

Cat's Claw, as treatment for
    viral infections, 74

CDC, 4, 69
    revised definition of
        CFIDS, 13-16

CEBV, 45
    common tests for, 49-50
    common treatment for, 51
    controversy over tests for,
        51
    description of antibodies
        during infection, 49
    diseases associated with, 48
    symptoms of, 46, 47
    wholistic remedies for, 52
    See also EBV; Viruses.

Centers for Disease Control
    and Prevention. *See* CDC.

CFIDS
    candidiasis and, 86

chemicals/heavy metals and, 119-120
CMV and, 54-55
dental amalgam and, 88
foamy retrovirus and, 66-67
HHV-6 and, 8, 60
mental illness and, 4, 14, 46
parasite infections and, 151-152
revised CDC definition of, 13-16
symptoms of allergies in, 112-113
viruses identified with, 44
Wilson's Syndrome and, 139-140
See also Downhill Syndrome, the.
Chelation therapy, 107-108
intravenous, 109
oral, 108-109
Chemicals
allergies to, 119-120
CFIDS and, 102, 119-120
commonly used, 101-102
elimination of, from body, 105-109
laws against use, 102-103
pervasiveness of, 95-96
potential dangers of, 100-101
sources of, 99
See also Allergies; Environmental illness;

Heavy metals.
Cheney, Dr. Paul R., 3-6, 51, 68, 69, 162
Choline, 108
Chronic Epstein-Barr Virus. *See* CEBV.
Chronic Fatigue and Immune Dysfunction Syndrome. *See* CFIDS.
Chronic Fatigue Associated Retrovirus Assay (CARA), 29-30
Chronic Fatigue Syndrome, 3. *See also* CFIDS; Downhill Syndrome, the.
CMV, 44
CFIDS and, 54-55
diagnosis of, 56
prevalence of, 53-54
tests for, 26-27, 28
three classical syndromes of, 55-56
treatment for, 56-57
Coenzyme Q_{10}, as treatment for viral infections, 74
Coxsackie virus, 21-23
Cytomegalovirus. *See* CMV.
Cytomegalovirus inclusion disease, 55.
Cytomegalovirus infection, acute acquired, 55

D

DeFreitas, Elaine, Ph.D., 5, 29, 65, 67, 68, 69
Detoxification
    chelation therapy, 107-109
    Hubbard method, 106-107
    liver, as part of treatment for MID, 40
    mercury, 92-93
Dieldrin, 101
Dientamoeba fragilis, 147. *See also* Protozoa.
Diet
    antiyeast (FAVER), 84-85
    healthy, as treatment for viral infections, 72-73
    See also Foods, organic.
Dilman, Professor Vladimir, 35, 36, 37-38
DNA, 43-44, 65, 66
Downhill Syndrome, the
    allergies as cofactors of, 111-120
    benefits of chelation therapy for, 107-109
    candidiasis as cofactor of, 79-86
    CEBV as cofactor of, 45-52
    chemicals as cofactors of, 95-103
    CMV as cofactor of, 53-57
    diagnostic tests for, 25-30
    early cases of, 3-8
    fatigue associated with, 11
    heavy metals as cofactors of, 95-103
    HHV-6 as cofactor of, 59-63
    hypothyroidism as cofactor of, 135-143
    mercury poisoning as cofactor of, 87-94
    MID and, 31-33, 35
    new information about, 162-163
    parasites as cofactors of, 145-157
    pleomorphism and, 20
    possible link with Sjogren syndrome, 62
    retroviruses as cofactor of, 65-69
    revised CDC definition of, 13-16
    role of nutrition and, 23
    signs and symptoms of, 12, 14-15
    viruses as possible cause of, 5
    See also CFIDS
Dresden, Florence, 85
Dysbiosis, 150-151

E

EBV, 44, 45
    as possible cause of the Downhill Syndrome, 4-5

tests for, 26-27, 28
See also CEBV.
EBV Panel test, 49
EBV-specific seriodiagnostic
tests, 50
Echinacea, as treatment for
viral infections, 75.
See also Medicine,
botanical; Herbs.
EDTA, 107, 109
Endosulfan, 101
Entamoeba coli, 147.
See also Protozoa.
Entamoeba histolytica, 146-147,
150, 151, 153
treatment of, 153-154
See also Protozoa.
Environmental illness, 111, 121
factors which predispose
people to, 120
See also Allergies;
Chemicals; Heavy metals.
Epstein-Barr virus. *See* EBV.

F

Fasting
procedures for, 125-126
to determine food allergies,
125
what to do after, 126
Fatigue, normal
differences between
Downhill Syndrome

fatigue and, 11-13
kinds of, 10-11
FAVER diet, 84-85
Fish oils, reversal of MID
with, 38-39
Foamy retroviruses, 66-67. *See
also* Retroviruses; Viruses.
Foods, organic, benefits of,
105-106

G

Gallagher, Mollie, 121-122
Galland, Leo, M.D., 150-152
Gantz, Nelson M., M.D., 13,
15, 23
Gastritis, 148-149
Giardia lamblia, 146-147, 150,
151
treatment of, 153
See also Protozoa.
Gittleman, Ann Louise, 148,
153
Glucagon, 38
Guess What Came to Dinner,
148, 153
Guiltinan, Jane, N.D., 40

H

Heart disease, ischemic, 37
Heavy metals
CFIDS and, 102

common exposures to, 97-99
effect of, on body, 96
elimination of, from body,
105-109
laws against use of, 102-103
pervasiveness of, 95-96
symptoms of poisoning,
97-99
See also Allergies;
Chemicals;
Environmental illness.
Helicobacter pylori, 149-150
treatment of, 155
See also Bacteria.
Helminth worms, 145, 146, 153
rise of, 147-148
treatment of, 154
See also Parasites.
Helper T cells, 27-29. *See also*
Lymphocytes.
Hemogram, 50
Hepatitis, 61
Herbs, as part of treatment for
MID, 40. *See also*
Medicine, botanical.
HIV, 5-6, 28. *See also* AIDS;
HTLV; Viruses.
Holmes, Dr. Gary, 4-5, 50, 51
Homeostasis, 17-18
as task of immune system,
32
HTLV, as possible cause of
CFIDS, 5-6, 68, 69
Hubbard, L. Ron, method of

detoxification, 106-107
Huggins, Hal A., D.D.S., 88,
94, 96
Human Herpesvirus DNA
Detection Assays, 26-27
Human Herpesvirus Type VI
(HHV-VI), 44
CFIDS and, 60
discovery of, 59-60
possible links with other
diseases, 61-62
tests for, 26-27
treatment of, 62-63
Human Herpesviruses (HHV),
26-27. *See also* CMV; EBV;
HHV-VI.
Human T-lymphotropic virus.
See HTLV.
Hyperglycemia, 33, 94
Hypoglycemia, 34, 94
Hyperinsulinemia, 33
Hypothalamus, 32
Hypothyroidism, cause of,
136. *See also* Wilson's
Syndrome.

I

IgG Subclasses Serum Level,
30
Immune system
effects of technology on,
19-20
factors which weaken, 18-19

five tasks of, 31-32
nutritional formulas for
boosting, 128-133
Immunogen, 114
Immunology, 31
Immunosuppression, 26, 28,
29
Incline Village, Nevada, 3, 4
Infusions, intravenous, as
treatment for viral
infections, 76
Insulin, 33, 35, 94
function of, 37
reversing MID by
regulation of, 36-38
Interferon, as treatment for
viral infections, 71-72. *See
also* Alpha-Interferon.
Interleukin-2, 28, 33
Interleukin-2 Serum Level, 28
Interleukin-6, 28-29
Interleukin-6 Serum Level, 28-
29
Ischemic heart disease, 37

J

Jessop, Carol, M.D., 39, 86

K

Kaplan, Jon, M.D., 4
Kelly, Kathleen, 157-159

Kelp, 108
Kennedy, Gerald, 10
Kepone, 101-102
Keshan disease, 23
Klimas, Nancy, Ph.D., 67-68
Komaroff, Anthony L., M.D.,
8, 51

L

Lead, 98
"Leaky gut" syndrome, 118
testing for, 127
See also Allergies.
Lectin, 151
Levy, Jay A., Ph.D., 67-68
Liver function tests, 50
Low-density lipoprotein
(LDL), 33, 35, 39
Lymphocyte Activated Killer
cells (LAK cells), 28
Lymphocyte Enumeration
Panel, 27-28
Lymphocyte Immune
Dysfunction Panel, 28
Lymphocytes, 25, 26, 27-29, 33,
35, 37, 39
Lyndonville, New York, 5-7

M

Macrophages, 29, 35, 39
Malathion, 102

Maleic Hydrazide, 102
MALIBU Test. *See* Mitogen-
    Activated Lymphocytes
    Test.
Maloney, Laura Ann, 35-36, 41
Marney, Samuel R., M.D., 119
Marshall, Barry, M.D.,
    149-150
Martin, W. John, M.D., Ph.D.,
    66-67
Medicines, botanical, as
    treatments for viral
    infections, 74-76. *See also*
    Herbs.
Mental illness, CFIDS and, 4,
    14, 46
Mercury
    detoxification of, 92-93
    toxicity of, 90
    See also Amalgam, dental;
    Heavy metals.
Mercury poisoning
    diagnosis of, 90-92
    signs and symptoms of, 87-
    88
    See also Amalgam, dental;
    Heavy metals.
Metabolic immunodepression.
    See MID.
Metabolism, 31
Metals, heavy. *See* Heavy
    metals.
MID
    as source of Downhill

Syndrome symptoms, 31
    description of, 32-34
    four major parameters of,
    35
    multi-level approach to
    treatment of, 40
    reversal of, using fish oils,
    38-39
    reversal of, using insulin,
    36-38
    six general treatment steps
    for reversing, 40-41
Minerals, as treatment for
    viral infections, 73-74
Mirex, 102
Mitogen-Activated
    Lymphocytes (MALIBU)
    Test, 26
Monolaurin, as treatment for
    viral infections, 74
Mononucleosis, 46, 48
    similarity of, to CFIDS, 3-4
    See also EBV.

N

National Institute of Allergy
    and Infectious Diseases
    (NIAID), 18
Natural Killer Cell
    Cytotoxicity Assay, 27
Natural Killer (NK) cells, 27, 28
Niacin, use of, for
    detoxification, 106-107.

See also Vitamins.
Nickel, 97

O

Omega-3 fatty acids, 38, 39

P

Pantothenic acid, 108
Parasites
    CFIDS and, 151-152
    definition of, 145-146
    diagnosis of, 152-153
    high incidence of infection,
        146-150
    symptoms of infection,
        150-151
    treatment of, 153, 155
Parrish, Dr. Louis, 150-151
Paul-Bunnell-Davidson test, 50
Peptic ulcer, 149
Phenformin, 37
Phenytoin, 38
Pleomorphism, 20-22
Pleva, Jaro, 88-89
Pollard, Alison, 7-8
Pollard, Hannah, 7
Pollard, Jean, 6-7
Pollard, Libby, 7
Pollard, Megan, 7
Pollutants, how to avoid, 103.
    See also Chemicals;
    Environmental illness;
    Heavy metals.
Polymerase chain reaction, 5
Preservatives, food, allergies
    to, 118-119. *See also*
    Allergies.
Protozoa, 145, 146
    effect of, on AIDS patients,
        151
    rise of, 146-148
    treatment of, 153-154
    See also Blastocystis hominis;
        Dientamoeba fragilis;
        Entamoeba coli; Entamoeba
        histolytica; Giardia lamblia;
        Parasites.
Provocative Neutralization
    Test, 128

R

Rapp, Doris J., M.D., 111-113
Retroviruses, 44, 65
    difference between viruses
        and, 66
    foamy, 66-67
See also Viruses.
Reverse transcriptase, 65, 66
Reynolds, Joyce, 9-10
RNA, 43-44, 65, 66
Roseola, 61
Rotary Diversified Diet, 126-
    127. *See also* Allergies.

S

Schmidt, Sandy, 9
Selenium, deficiency of
    coxsackie virus and, 21-22
    Keshan disease and, 23
Serial Dilution Endpoint
    Titration, 128
Shields, Megan G., M.D., 106-
    107
Sjogren syndrome, possible
    link with CFIDS, 62
Soluble CD-8 Receptor Level,
    29
Soluble CD-23 Receptor Level,
    29
Soluble Interleukin-2 Receptor
    Level, 28
Sundberg, Donna Kay, 159-160
Supressor T cells, 27-29. *See
    also* Lymphocytes.

T

Thyroid
    function of, 135-136
    underactive, as cofactor of
        the Downhill Syndrome,
        135-143
    See also Hypothyroidism;
        Wilson's Syndrome.
Thyroid-stimulating hormone
    (TSH), 136
Thyrotropin-releasing

hormone (TRH), 136
Thyroxine (T_4), 135-136
Triglycerides, high levels of
    mercury toxicity and, 94
    MID and, 37, 38, 39
Triiodothyronine (T_3), 135-136
    as treatment for Wilson's
        Syndrome, 140

V

Valencia, Jessica, 160-161
Viruses
    as cofactors of the
        Downhill Syndrome,
        43-44
    as possible cause of CFIDS,
        5
    composition of, 43-44
    difference between
        retroviruses and, 66
    holistic remedies for, 72-76
    interferon as treatment for,
        71-72
    pleomorphism and, 21-23
    See also AIDS; CMV;
        Coxsackie virus; EBV;
        HIV; HTLV; Human
        Herpesviruses;
        Retroviruses.
Vitamins, as treatments for
    viral infections, 73

W

Warren, Robin, M.D., 149
Wilson, E. Denis, M.D., 136
Wilson's Syndrome, 136-137
    CFIDS and, 139-140
    diagnosis of, 137-139
    reversal of, naturally, 141-143
    T_3 therapy as treatment for, 140

Wonstad, Lydia, 45-46
Worms, helminth. *See* Helminth worms.

Y

Yanick, Paul, Jr., Ph.D., 31

Healthy Habits

are easy to come by—
If You Know Where to Look!

To get the latest information on:
- better health • diet & weight loss
- the latest nutritional supplements
- herbal healing & homeopathy and more

COMPLETE AND RETURN THIS CARD RIGHT AWAY!

Where did you purchase this book?

- ❏ bookstore
- ❏ supermarket
- ❏ health food store
- ❏ other (please specify)_____
- ❏ pharmacy

Name _____

Street Address _____

City _____ State _____ Zip _____

Trying to eat healthier? Looking to lose weight? Frustrated with bland-tasting fat-free foods?

For more information on how you can create low-fat meals that are packed with taste and nutrition and develop healthy habits that can improve the quality of your life,

COMPLETE AND RETURN THIS CARD!

Where did you purchase this book?

- ❏ bookstore
- ❏ supermarket
- ❏ health food store
- ❏ other (please specify)_____
- ❏ pharmacy

Name _____

Street Address _____

City _____ State _____ Zip _____

Complete and return this card for a FREE copy of HEALTHIER TIMES!

AVERY PUBLISHING GROUP

120 Old Broadway

Garden City Park, NY 11040

COMPLETE AND RETURN THIS CARD FOR A FREE COPY OF HEADED FOR SUCCESS!

AVERY PUBLISHING GROUP

120 Old Broadway

Garden City Park, NY 11040